I0682897

The New E.R.A.

K. McCoy

Published by be a muse productions, LLC, 2024.

The New E.R.A.
By K. McCoy
Written Work by K. McCoy
Copyright © 2024, All rights reserved.

This is a work of fiction. Names, characters, places, and incidents either are the product of the author's imagination or are used fictitiously. Any resemblance to actual persons, living or dead, events, or locales is entirely coincidental.

⬦ 2024 K. McCoy

First Edition: 2024

For permissions, inquiries, or other requests, please contact:
www.authorkmccoy.com

THE NEW E.R.A.

First edition. October 8, 2024.

ISBN: 979-8991737647

Written by K. McCoy.

To every reader and TV show fan that screamed for justice for their favorite Black supernatural characters, this is for you.

THE LAST TEST

Ya'll done tested us for the last muthafuckin' time!
Ripped Roots - Pam
Rage Uprisings - Jael
Rules - Jael

Ripped Roots

Pam

A SPLITTING HEADACHE, far worse than any mirage, made opening my eyes difficult. But the deafening silence had me shook, as I finally did. The pitch black darkness that greeted me was hella confusing too. Shaking my head, my locs felt heavy with each slight movement, as if I'd just finished co-washing them.

My whole body ached, and all I wanted was to go home and see my baby. *Damn, how long was I out?*

The last thing I remembered was a bunch of lanky dudes hovering around me in white coats inside a room. My mind flashed back to them hooking me up to a bunch of machines and using words I knew I wouldn't remember, along with a nurse who stuck me with a needle. The searing pain that followed right after the injection was something straight out of a nightmare.

My senses were coming back to me slowly, as my nose was being assaulted by what I could only describe as hot shit. Focusing on twitching my fingers, then toes, until I could lift my arms, I crept around in the dark. I could hardly get a good grip on the ground below. The soft wetness underneath me was not stable, and my feet fell through a few times before I could crawl around.

I have to get up.

Blinking my eyes in hopes of seeing even a flicker of light, I continued crawling on my hands and knees until I came to a hard stop. With my right hand, I took my time sweeping around the space. A blast of air brushed along my clammy fingers, causing my heart to pick up in pace as hope surged through my chest. Pushing the rest of my body upward, I ignored the pain that shot up through my lower back. I took in a few more harsh breaths, each one worse than the last, before bringing myself to the other side.

Where am I?

The silence that surrounded me was weird as hell. Growing up in the city, I got used to always hearing cars and music blasting from somebody's house, no matter what time of day or night it was. Closing my eyes, I tried focusing harder to see what else I could remember from the last several hours. Nothing came to mind and it was pissing me off.

Why can't I remember what happened to me?

Heat sped from my chest to my face, and I opened my eyes again. Looking down from where I was before, hot tears soon blurred my vision.

Bodies on top of bodies stared back at me. Some looked like they were sleeping, others had their eyes wide open. The one thing they all shared was being covered in blood.

My stomach was burning up now, and when my knees buckled, I had no more energy to keep them up. On the ground, I took another quick breath and when I did, the wind blew the scent that I had smelled before back toward me at the same time. The tears fell as bile rushed out of my mouth, splashing onto the ground near my bent knees.

Flashes of light made my eyes burn and memories came back to back - the boiling feeling inside my head that spread down my body, screams, the lanky men in white rushing toward me. My arm tingled, and I grabbed it, remembering the towering six men that held me down and the nurse stabbing me in the arm.

After that, I can't remember anything else. Though now I could focus more clearly on my surroundings and soon realized that I wasn't too far away from home. But without my car or money, getting there was going to take some work.

I have to go home.

Staring down at the ground next to me, the bodies spread out over the distance of two parked semi trucks, my hands balled up into fists. *I can't believe this! How could they do this to people?*

Even finding out that I had stage three breast cancer two months prior didn't hurt as much as seeing the sight in front of me. My mama died when me and Tammy were in high school from the same thing, so we knew the chances were high for us getting taken out by the same too someday. But this - this was different. *It was supposed to be a vaccine!*

I could feel the heat building up in my body, and my stomach growled. I always wanted something to eat when I got angry, but this wasn't the time. Standing up again, I looked down at my dirty and bloody tank top and jeans. Something white in the stark night caught my eye. A white wristband around my right arm with the words Green, P. - female - 717023 had been typed on the thin band. Ripping the wristband off my arm and stuffing it into my pockets, I trudged forward.

I can't let baby girl and Tammy see me like this.

THE NEAREST BUILDING was the medical center where I signed up to take the vaccine. Just looking at it made me angrier. Tammy told me not to do it, but when that suit showed up at the hospital to promote the vaccine, they said their firm would pay for all my future medical bills and take care of my baby girl until she was an adult, I couldn't say no. I signed those papers so fast, and look what it got me - tossed into a pit with a bunch of other desperate folks.

The first step back on solid ground hurt like a bitch, with my whole body burning and aching. Ain't no telling what them lab rats stuck in my arm. Looking inside the pixie glass doors, I couldn't see anything—not even an emergency light flickered inside. Everything appeared to have been shut down. My ears picked up the sound of sirens, so I followed it.

After a mile, the sound was gone, but the need to eat wasn't. My breathing was heavy, and I could barely keep my eyes open.

I kept to the back roads so no one would see me, but the closer I got to a fast food spot, I didn't care who saw me. Hearing the blaring music of a car behind me, I wish I had stayed hidden.

"Hey baby. Where you going?"

I ignored the SUV and looked around. There wasn't no one else around, at least from what I could see.

"Damn, you don't hear me talking to you?"

With my stomach and lungs on fire, I prayed they'd find somewhere else to be.

"Yo bitch! Answer when I speak to you!"

I paused and closed my eyes, taking a deep breath. As I did, warm saliva filled my mouth. The metallic taste was so good, I brought my lips inward to get more of its flavor. My breathing deepened as my body registered and rejoiced in the liquid traveling within my body. Each of my veins singed as saliva went from warm to hot while it unfurled quickly, like a quiet fire to both the tips of my fingers and the soles of my feet. As much as it thrilled me, this unique sensation also surprised me. Opening my eyes quickly, I saw not one, but three dudes staring at me.

"Man, let's just go. She looked damaged anyway." The guy on the passenger side said.

The creaking groans from the back door to their ride grabbed my attention. That was when I realized all the other noises that I could hear. At first it was a muffled sound, but with each second that passed, the noises became clearer. One soon stood out above the others - a slow, stretching sound, like wrapping tape around a package. I turned my head, and even though I couldn't see him, once the door to their ride slammed shut, my intuition ranged loud - telling me that the dude from the other side was making his way toward me.

"What happen to yo ass? Ya old man put you out?"

While the two men in the SUV laughed, I fought a wave of hunger that came from the clear view of the veins in their necks while the one outside the SUV stalked closer.

What the hell is wrong with me?!

Taking another inhale, I rotated my neck and murmured, "Leave me alone."

One dude whistled low, in a dark taunting tone, causing my arms to tremble. "You hear her dawg? Talking all big!"

"Right? She must can't count, cause last I checked, there was more of us here."

My flight responses were on high alert the second I saw the guy up close. He had a blade in his hand and a sick grin on his face. "Oh, we'll leave you alone, soon as we done withcha."

I tried to step back slowly to make a run for it, but he was faster. When he grabbed my arm, his smile wavered. "Damn! Let's toss this one back - she smells like shit!"

"Nah! We ain't seen no one else out here in days. Just put her in the back on the tarp."

My vision got blurry for a second, but in a blink of an eye, everything around me snapped into crystal clear view.

Even my hearing felt like it was surround sound as I heard and spotted the detailed brown and white feathers on two birds as they flapped away in a hurry from a tree branch. I tried to kick him to get free, but with a good few inches on me, he gripped my arm even tighter. Finally, I released a scream and the dude's hand came down hard across my face. The taste of my blood didn't scare me. It was the need for more that did.

"Let me go!" I shouted.

Panic settled in further to my body when he dragged me toward the back of the SUV. I could feel my skin growing hotter. When he turned me around, I saw the plastic tarp on the ground and a roll of dark duct tape. The gleam from the moonlight made the knife next to a box of condoms that much easier to recognize.

With my free hand, I dug my trembling fingernails into his face.

"Ugh! You bitch!"

A trickle of blood dripped down his face, and surprising myself, I licked my lips. When he reached out to hit me again, I was ready. Crouching low like the instructor at the Y taught us, I shielded my face with my forearm. I kicked him as hard as I could in the shin and blinked several times as I heard a bone break.

We toppled to the ground, with me landing on top of him, my mouth just above his neck. I could hear his ragged breathing and zeroed in on the pulsing vein. I pressed a hand on his face and shoulder, pinning him down. Throwing my head back, my skull felt like it was being dunked into molten lava. A cry ripped through me before I felt a razor sharp pain shoot from inside the gums of my teeth. My new thirst and instincts overrode my logic, propelling my head down to the thick vein that called out to me.

Warm blood filled my mouth, and no matter how much I tried to tell myself not to, I kept taking in more. Feeling the body underneath me wither and gasping for air only urged me to suck harder.

"What the fuck?"

My lips parted from his neck as my head snapped to the sound from behind. I growled and quickly swatted at the shaking hand of the guy beneath me. With my eyes still on the second guy from the SUV, I thought back to what they had planned to do.

Rage took over my hands, and as the thought flashed through my mind, I felt his neck snap. His body went still before his hand even touched the concrete.

Two more guys jumped out of the SUV, each with a gun in their hands. My eyes widened when I heard two small churns, followed by a fast crack. Gripping the shirt and waistband of his baggy jeans, I sent their boy flying toward them.

"Oh HELL nah!"

Hard stomps pounded against the concrete as one guy took off in the opposite direction. Bullets buzzed above my head, but none landed on me. When I had another thought to reach for one of their necks, I was in their face in seconds. The feel of their racing pulse around my hand felt so good, I instantly wet my lips in anticipation. A small whimper reached my ears, and I cut my eyes at the other guy. His eyes were on me, and I wrinkled my nose at the smell of urine.

Keeping my grip on the guy's throat, I took a quick look at their ride. A black Tahoe with spinners was almost considered lame where I'm from, but I needed to get home. I stretched open my mouth and felt the sharp edges of my teeth scrape the insides of my cheeks.

"Where are the keys?"

"Wh-what?"

"Give me the keys to the Tahoe."

"Fu—"

I cut off more of his air supply as his friend reached into the pocket of their jeans. He tossed the keys at me, and in a flash, they were in my other hand. The hunger wasn't as bad as it was before, but I still wanted more. Shaking my head, I thought back to what I did minutes ago.

"Please don't kill me! I'm somebody's son!" the guy in front of me pleaded.

"Ain't I somebody? Somebody's daughter? Sister? Mama?" I choked out, as thoughts of my baby girl entered my mind.

My head cocked over to the guy that I held up midair. He was wheezing and turning blue, but I refused to let him go. *How many others did they do this shit to?*

"I-I sorry! Please! Don't kill me sister!"

"Oh, now I'm ya sister? Ain't that a bitch?"

I let the guy in my grasp go and stared down as he took in big shaky breaths. My body still ached, but not as much as it did when I left the clinic. I walked over to the driver's side of the Tahoe and climbed into the driver's seat. The engine rumbled when I turned the ignition and drove away.

With the night breeze cooling me down, I reached for the tuners and searched for a radio station. Finding TNT 109.1 FM, I made a soft left turn and turned the volume up.

Y'all are tuning in to the Twerk and Tell hotline, where we play the tracks you twerk to and tell you what's treading while it's hot!

The local news is still advising everyone to stay indoors, with more wild ass reports of people being attacked on the streets by the unhoused. So y'all lock up, strap up, and stay blessed up - ya heard!

Instead of hearing more news, TNT played a popular club throwback, so at the next light, I switched the station. Once I found one talking about the vaccine, I parked the car in a vacant lot and rolled up the windows. The smell of cannabis grew stronger, but I needed to give my attention to whatever they were saying, so I left them up and focused.

...Each medical faculty known to be involved in the most recent vaccine against the DELTA V variant, medically called the Essential Radioactive Antigen, that is now commonly being referred to as the E.R.A, have been shut down. The rising death toll is now in the hundreds of thousands. Families of those affected are demanding the company behind the vaccine, Lee Henry Ko-Ops, take responsibility and are also seeking to take legal action. Since the closing of all medical faculties, a series of random and seriously violent attacks are being reported throughout the city.

We will continue to provide you all with more news here on WXDO...

I rested my head back on the headrest once I turned off the radio. After taking in a few deep breaths and almost gagging on the smell inside the car, I started rummaging around the passenger side of the car. Out of habit, I went to turn on the middle light and narrowed my eyes when every wrapper and fast food cup on the floor came into view. I followed the sides of the small glove compartment until I felt a seam of tape at the very top. With my fingernails, I picked at it until the black tape came up and I pulled it down. Stacks and stacks of cash soon stared back at me.

"Well, shit." I breathed out.

Taking another deep inhale, I closed my eyes and when my nose cut through the engine oil, metallics, cheap perfume, and stale black and milds, my hands itched.

I should've ended all their asses.

It was faint, but I would know that smell anywhere. Burnt plastic and aluminum foil mingled with cocaine cooked twice over was the scent of my childhood. At least until mama finally kicked daddy out for the last time.

Crawling to the back of the seat, I scanned the space until I found a duffel bag big enough to put the cash in. Once I unzipped it, more street pharmaceuticals toppled out. Before I became too angry to see straight, I grabbed a soiled t-shirt from the floor and dumped all the contents onto it. The last thing to fall out from the bottom of the bag were more stacks, so I picked those up and put them back inside the bag. Adding the other stacks from the glove compartment, I took another glance at everything I'd emptied out.

Remembering what my mama did years ago, I tied the t-shirt as tight as I could and fumbled around for a lighter so I could burn and chuck that poison the first chance I got.

As I tossed the bag full of cash in the seat next to me, a low vibration sound buzzed from the back seat. But I ignored it while cranking back up the engine and tuning in to the local news on the radio.

Police have received an alarming number of reports of people being attacked by others under the influence of a new street drug known as Dog Scraps, or DS for short. We were able to secure footage of an attack that occurred less than an hour ago, but we must warn you, the video recording is disturbing and not suitable for young viewers. Images of said attacks are now available on our website, but please view with caution, as the images are extremely graphic. Stay tuned to WXDO as we continue to update you with the latest breaking news.

"Mama's coming home, baby girl." I whispered while stepping on the gas pedal.

TWO SOLID HOURS OF driving and I could barely keep my eyes open. As I turned down the street to my neighborhood, the quietness had me double checking the streets to make sure everything was alright. It wasn't until I passed the local Jamaican restaurant, the bright pink building with murals of Rita Marley and the owners on the side, did I start to calm down. Some shops in the plaza across from the restaurant had boarded up their windows. The phone in the backseat had been vibrating nonstop for the last hour, so before turning down the street to the house I shared with my sister, I parked the SUV to check it.

Text after text from someone named BBG came across the screen. Each one ended with a question.

Where u at?

Why u ain't answerin me?

U got my shit?

Where u at wit my shit?

This must be who those fools worked for.

While I was reading the rest of the messages, one came through with an image that made me freeze. It was a picture of the guy I drained. Now that I was out of the situation, seeing what I had done should have made me sick to my stomach. Instead, I felt saliva gather in my mouth again. That was until another message popped up on the screen.

We gon find u bitch.

Rolling my eyes, I went back to the picture. And the longer I stared at the picture, the more I remembered the taste of his blood as it coated my throat. The incisors of my teeth extended, piercing my bottom lip. Soon the scent of sweet rust had me swiping my tongue across the lip and my eyes widened when I let out a small moan.

What is happening to me?

Glancing down at the phone still in my hand, I clicked on the web search engine and typed in 'E.R.A.'. Images flooded the screen, along with video. I clicked on the first video, the screams that came after rooted me to the spot. A woman could be seen running through a small crowd, but she tripped and while trying to get up, a figure leaped forward, landing on top of her. The people in the crowd shouted and scattered. Whoever was recording the footage kept their distance while zooming in on the woman, whose blood curdling screams drowned out everyone else.

If there was no sound, anyone looking at the video would think it was just two drunks making out in the middle of the street. Until one of the woman's bloody hands came into view. A shoe flew in the air, almost hitting the figure on top of the screaming woman. The bloody figure turned and caught the show mid-air. With her face twisted, she snarled, and soon her eyes locked onto whoever was recording the video. Dropping the other woman to the ground, the snarling woman sprinted toward the camera person just before the video ended.

With a shaking hand, I pressed rewind on the screen and paused it on the part where that exposed the figure's face. Seeing a woman who looked like she could've passed for my baby sister attacking someone like that filled me with so much fear. I dropped the phone in my lap and tried to steady my breathing as I started the ride again.

My house was in clear view as I drove, but as I went to turn into the driveway, a tiny light shone from one room upstairs. A cloud sign that spelled out 'Kem's Korner' hung on the wall, with posters of boy bands covering the closet door. Just above the cloud sign was the stethoscope I got baby girl for her 16th birthday last year. My throat grew tight when I remembered my girl telling me she wanted to study medicine in college after coming home that summer from volunteering at the YMCA. I had spent years working as a CNA to provide for us, and to know my child would one day succeed where I failed filled me with pride.

I stared at the image in front of me, clear as can be of my baby girl, dancing in her room with Tammy, both with big smiles on their faces. The last thing I saw was Tammy pulling baby girl into her arms.

My vision blurred as I kept driving straight ahead. I didn't stop until I was a few stop signs away from the house. Seeing my baby so happy - and safe - without me kept the tears sliding down my face. More images of what I did earlier tonight now clashed with memories I had with my baby girl. From taking care of her when she was sick, to her first steps, to the last time I kissed her cheek when I left to go to the medical center. I rested my head on the steering wheel and let the pain wash over me.

"I'm so sorry, baby girl. I can't come back to you like this."

When I brought my head up, I caught a glimpse of myself in the rearview mirror. The red tear stains were all the confirmation I needed to stay away from the only family I have left in this world. It was the best way I knew to protect them.

I put my foot on the gas pedal and drove away from home for the last time.

Rage Uprisings

Jael

I PULLED UP IN MY '98 white Camry to the neon pink building I overheard some girls talking about at the 24-hour diner. It wasn't hard to find, with every other place boarded up as I drove steadily down each block after leaving the diner. Grabbing the half eaten muffin I splurged on earlier, I polished it off while looking around at the building in front of me.

"This can't be the spot they work at."

But I knew it was the strip club they worked at once I saw the name the girls kept shouting in the diner scribbled in bright pink on the double black doors.

A neon pink light flashed on above the two large black double doors, with the name Smackz. Bass speakers blared behind me, and I adjusted the rearview mirror to see who else was coming. A shiny lime green Cadillac rumbled next to my ride, and four chicks hopped out, each already dressed for auditions in their white and neon floss.

The shortest one from the entourage walked up to the window of my car and whipped her 40 inch wavy bundles against the window. "Ya ain't gonna make no stacks starin' shawty! Get out and show us whatcha workin' with!"

"You wild as fuck Kitty!"

The girls cackled as Kitty sashayed back over to them. Taking one last look at the scrapbook in the passenger seat, I removed the keys from the ignition before opening the door and stepping out.

More cars pulled into the gravel parking lot as I jogged to catch up to the others. Once I was inside, the blast of cold air hit me and I saw the girls from earlier sitting at the bar signing a clipboard. A white woman sporting a long French braid and wearing clear high heels surveyed us quietly. When she strolled over toward the center of the room, I straightened my posture once I saw that she towered over my five foot six-inch frame.

"I'm Gwen. Y'all all here for the auditions?" she asked.

Kitty smacked her teeth before mumbling, "Nah, we just wearing floss for fun."

Gwen's eyes scanned the group, and a smirk spread across her oval face as she pointed a long, black acrylic nail at Kitty. "You can bounce. "

"What?"

"You not auditioning today. Leave."

"You ain't serious!"

Kitty glared up and down at Gwen. Malice filled her voice when she asked, "Who you think you talking to, Becky?"

"If I have to repeat myself, I'll tell you again with my right hook."

I watched as Kitty jumped off the bar stool and ran up to Gwen. But before Kitty could reach her, another woman appeared from behind and lifted her up from the ground. She easily had almost a foot in height on Kitty, with dark russet brown skin and the meanest mug I'd seen in a minute. Even in the dim light, the diamonds from her open faced fanged grillz glimmered as she growled low. Several of the girls that arrived with Kitty backed up without a word.

I blinked as the woman sent rapid slaps to Kitty's bare ass, each time muttering something I couldn't make out. Kitty's friends each began to make their way to the door once Kitty dropped to the floor. The long bundles covered Kitty's face, but her whimpering echoed throughout the room.

"I'm hungry and ain't got time for this shit!" The woman who dropped Kitty to the floor announced.

"Sorry boss, I'll wrap this up."

"Good." Sneering down at Kitty's trembling body, the woman barked, "Keep cryin', and I'll sink my teeth into your 'lil ass!"

Seeing the woman's fangs again, this time even closer than before. I willed myself to stay still while staring down at the floor.

It'd been four months since the news of the E.R.A. vaccine disaster went worldwide, along with those that survived. But this was the first time I'd been in a room with one of them.

Kitty's hand went over her mouth as she choked back a sob. After a minute of silence, she finally stood and scurried next to her friends to leave. The bright morning light spilled inside the building for a second before the double doors slammed shut.

The woman Gwen called boss surveyed the rest of us before glancing at Gwen. They nodded at one another, and the taller woman ran her tongue over her front teeth. When she blurred out of sight behind a dark curtain, the other girls slowly made their way to the bar, and I let out the breath I forgot I was holding. Gwen walked behind the bar, picked up a shot glass, and filled it to the brim with a deep brown liquid from a nearby bottle. Bringing the shot glass to her lips, Gwen tilted her head back as she knocked back the booze in one go. She then stared hard at us, slamming the glass down onto the bar counter.

"Smackz is one of the last titty joints not full of pimps and strung out girls for a reason. You wanna get ya stacks and go home in one piece? You do what we say, and we'll protect y'all with our last breath."

A few girls whispered while Gwen poured herself another shot. "We ain't got many other rules. Smackz gets a lot of ERAs in here, so you gotta be cool with that. And if you need a little somethin' somethin' to take the stage, you can take your ass home now. We ain't losing our license cause ya can't piss in a cup. It's one of the last legal tactics that the old government still has, and if all the boarded-up buildings 'round here ain't tell you already, they real quick to use that shit to shut us down. Or worse - let a group of dudes who'll pay for city dog protection in cash take over. "

A door creaked open as uptempo music boomed inside the club. Two more women, both giggling and chatting together, walked in. They both wore black sneakers and mid length neon pink coats. With their micro braids and sister locs pulled back in one long, low ponytail, I watched as the taller one removed her coat. My mouth dropped as I stared down at her curvy, thick frame while the shorter woman skipped over to Gwen and took away her shot glass.

As the taller woman with a deep midnight complexion strolled by me and reached out her hand to her head, freeing the micro braids she rocked, the scent of fresh roses followed and I questioned my sexuality on site when she caught me looking and winked.

"These the newbies, Gwen?" The girl next to Gwen asked, sipping on a drink.

Gwen sighed before putting away the bottle. "Maybe. They haven't taken the stage yet."

"Yea! We get a show before work!"

"You wiped down everything from last night, Gwen?"

"I did, as always."

The taller woman stopped next to the bar and removed her boots as Gwen handed her a pair of neon pink heels.

"I'm Tam with da Yams. And if ya can do half of what I can do, ya might be able to make a stack or two tonight."

Looking straight at me, she grinned and slinked onto the stage. When her hands reached the first pole, Tam leaned forward and swung around twice before stopping and whining down until her ass grazed the floor. She came back up in fluid motion before climbing the silver pole. With her legs gripping it in a scissor formation, Tam inched down, following the rhythmic beat of the music while caressing her breasts with one hand and swatting her ass with the other.

"Get it! Get it Tam!"

"Ain't no way I can do that."

"She just showing off..."

When her heels touched the ground, Tam gripped the brass bar, swinging around the pole again, this time hooking one of her legs as she twirled and landed softly in a split on the stage. Tam's hands then roamed over her lush hourglass frame, pausing to give each breast a gentle squeeze while moving her ass cheeks to the synthesized drums and loud bass line music.

Gwen stepped from behind the bar with two silver buckets, placing one at the front of the stage and handing Tam the other. With her eyes on each of us, Gwen smirked.

"Once Tam wipes down, you each get to show us what you got. The vet girls will vote on your potential talent, and if you make it through, you get a $200 advance to pick out your new floss and heels for tonight. Good luck."

* * *

I stared at my reflection in the mirror, taking in the Bantu twists I whipped up before taking the stage. The sparkly sky blue floss I chose made my warm beige skin pop, just like Tam said it would. Still can't believe I made it past the first audition, and with just $36 dollars left to my name, I'm glad that I did.

A few girls left to get something to eat from the food truck that was setting up, but something about having tortas before my first shift didn't sound right. So I hung back, grabbed a bottle of water, and stuck a crippled up dollar bill into the vending machine. While chewing on the peanut butter crackers, I closed my eyes and took a sip of water. Flashes of the last few months crossed my mind, and I could feel the tears threatening to leave my eyes.

Everyone I knew was gone, except Amanda. As soon as I have enough stacks saved up, I'mma leave and make my way to PA. That's where her moms said she was heading before the anti-ERA rednecks in town fucked everything up.

"Nervous, newbie?"

I followed the voice and found the girl who came in earlier with Tam staring at me. We were almost the same height, even though she already was rocking a pair of baby pink platform heels.

"Honestly? Hell yeah."

"Everyone gets a little nervous the first time, don't sweat it. I'm Keki," she told me. "Tamira - I mean, Tam with da Yam's my cousin."

"Tam's your cousin?"

"Yeah, yeah, I know. My cuz been a baddie since we was jits."

We shared a laugh, and Keki bumped her hip against mine. "Let's go and chill with the others."

I nodded as she led the way back to the front of the club. When we stepped through the dressing room curtain, I saw the boss standing at the podium where we entered, counting several bills. When she snarled I reached for Keki's elbow.

"What's up, newbie?"

I quickly glanced at the boss again before asking, "Um, the boss straight, right?"

"Whatcha mean?"

"You know, like, she ain't hungry no more? Cause I don't wanna get on her bad side and end up on the menu."

Keki laughed. "Oh, you got jokes." She glanced over at the boss and shook her head. "Her name's Ebony. She's good, just ornery as hell."

"How did she end up an ERA?" I found myself asking.

Keki shook her head and sat in a chair at the front of the main stage. I joined her, and she looked behind as more girls did the same. "Her bum ass boyfriend. He used to own this place. When Ebony returned from the dead, word is she came back and found him sticking it to some boney bitch who went by Sapphire. They say she drained both they asses and took over the club the same night."

"Damn."

"Yeah. That was before me and Tam got here, but Gwen was here when it went down. Ask her if you wanna know more."

"Nah, I'm good."

Hearing the clanking of heels from behind, I turned around to see Ebony watching us. I knew she heard us when her eyes met mine and her fangs popped out. My whole body froze, and she laughed.

"Now that y'all flossed up, don't forget what Gwen and them told ya. All newbies rotate the front door for an hour each. Y'all only doing tag team dances after taking the stage, and if Gwen says do something - do it."

Two other new girls looked over at Ebony, and one of them lowered her head before nudging the other. I watched as they whispered to one another and Ebony rolled her eyes as Gwen shouted from the bar.

"Speak up newbie!"

"Y-you the mother here?" one of them finally asked.

Ebony squinted her eyes while glancing over at the girls. "Who the fuck is Mother?"

"Y'all haven't heard of Mother? She runs three safe houses down in the south for ERA-ers." one of them explained.

Keki's head snapped over to the girls. "Oh yeah! I heard of her. My ex from Florida say she bad as fuck. Said she even cleaned out a whole town of dope dealers in one night."

"Yeah! That's Mother," the girl confirmed with a head nod.

Ebony scoffed. "That's some bullshit. Ain't no sister doing all that."

The girl who spoke first looked at Keki and twirled the ends of her wavy curls. "Word is she mostly keeps to herself, but got a soft spot for the young ERAs that can't go back home."

Her friend peeked up at Ebony and sat up straight when Ebony narrowed her eyes. "They say that's why she started running the shelters for the young ERAs and other kids that need a place to stay."

Keki and I nodded while Ebony scoffed. "Whatever, keep ya fairy tales out my spot. The folks that roll up in here only wanna see the fantasy."

One newbie whispered, "Yeah, she ain't no mother."

Ebony whipped her head toward the girl and snapped, "And don't you forget it! I'm only interested in you handing me my cut after your shifts - got it?"

When the girls all looked at one another and then the floor, Ebony barked, "You fuckin' heard me, so speak!"

A few mumbled as the girl closest to her answered,"Yes."

"Good. Doors open in 30 minutes."

* * *

My first week at Smackz went by so fast, I barely had time to stress about still living out of my car. So far, no one from the club noticed. I was always the first to give Ebony my cut for the night, and after tucking half my earnings into a shoe box inside my locker, I drove up to the 24-hour laundromat a few blocks away to wash my clothes and sleep. But when I stepped outside after my last shift, some dudes pulled up next to my car. Their windows were tinted and rolled up, but that didn't stop smoke from making its way out of the old F-450. I knew I couldn't go back to the laundromat tonight, so on my way out I thought about what I'd have for dinner at the diner.

"Everything good, Jael?"

Wilma, the closing security for the night, marched over to me. It didn't take long for her to place a hand on my shoulder to pull me back while she looked outside. We were the same height, but as I listened to the dog tags around her neck rattle under the long sleeve black tee and bulletproof vest she wore, I didn't dare put up a fight. Wilma brought her right hand across my chest, and my eyes widened as she removed her gun from the holster.

"Stay here," she commanded while glaring straight ahead. Pressing a hand to the earpiece in her left ear, Wilma gripped the small black firearm with both hands and kept it low.

"Rana. I got four - five bodies out front."

"On it."

Before the front door closed, I saw a figure move fast toward the parking lot. I then heard glass shatter and more loud noises, but with Wilma in front of me, all I could focus on was her pushing me back inside the main room. Even with my heart picking up speed, I couldn't help but look up at her. Wilma was the more quiet one of the security guards at Smackz. Besides a subtle head nod every once in a while, I hardly noticed her. So I took in her fair olive skin and light green eyes while Wilma's glare remained straight ahead.

Soon we heard tires screeching, and Wilma placed her gun back in its holster.

Without the music or people talking inside the club, every little noise felt amplified. I wondered if this is what it was like for an ERA on the daily until I felt a gust of wind float up to the back of my neck. Ebony's voice was low, but I could still hear the annoyance in her tone when she spoke.

"Everything good out here?"

Wilma stood even straighter when she answered, "Yeah, boss. We good."

"Then why fresh meat here ain't on her way to the laundromat?"

My throat went dry as I tried to think of something to say. "Wh-who..."

"We know 'bout you sleepin' in your ride." Gwen confirmed while strolling in from the back entrance with Rana.

"How long y'all known?" I asked, my voice barely above a whisper.

I wanted to crawl into a hole in the ground when Ebony's laughter reached my ears. "Day one, fresh meat. Figured with a few stacks, you'd at least get a hotel." She used one of her long, coffin shaped nails to pick in between her fangs. "Must be down bad to sleep out in that shit."

"Boss, go easy on her. She don't know nobody here." Wilma explained.

Ebony instead sucked in her teeth. "All the 'mo reason for her ass not to be out there! Hell, you been going up there to watch over her for days now, and I ain't payin' you extra to play bodyguard with her 'lil ass."

"Rana got the drop on the bodies out front. They local." Gwen interrupted.

Sitting down in a chair near the main stage, my eyes went to Rana as she took off her boots. The loud thump reminded me of thunder just before a storm. From the corner of my eye, I could see Ebony as she joined Gwen behind the bar. The two quietly restocked and wiped down the counter.

"So, it's safe to say we ain't the only ones that know about your situation, newbie." Rana said before adding, "The question is, what we do about it now?"

"She can stay with us, right, boss?" Gwen asked aloud.

The thought of trying to get a good night's sleep while under the same roof as Ebony made me speak up. Turning to face the two women, I cleared my throat. "Uh, th-thank you for the offer, but I wouldn't feel right taking up space with my bosses."

"But you cool with sleepin' out in the open?" Ebony challenged, "Where any and everybody could snatch ya ass up and leave ya in the back of a dumpster?"

"Boss!" Wilma shouted.

Ebony zipped past me in a blur and stood in front of Wilma. Both had their fangs out, and I took two steps back.

"You and I both know what's out there, and fresh meat here actin' like they ass was pushed out yesterday." Ebony snarled. "You wanna protect her? Then get her ass up to speed 'fore one of us get smoked tryna save a ho!"

Rana slid down from her bar stool and mumbled something under her breath. I couldn't hear what it was, but when Ebony's head darted toward Rana, the glare she set on Rana almost made me piss myself.

"You got something to say, Rana?"

"Nah, Boss."

"Then why you reaching for your steels?"

"Cause they need cleaning."

Soft clanking sounds were heard as Rana removed three knives, each different sizes, from the sheathed pockets around the right thigh of her cargo pants. Gwen huffed while shaking her head, filling a small red bucket with water and dish soap. Dropping a sponge inside the bucket, she placed it on top of the bar counter toward Rana. Without a word, Rana wiped the blades gently from top to bottom with the small sponge, setting each knife down on the bar counter.

"Newbie, them boys had your plate number." Rana calmly stated. "And two of them had pictures of you inside your car on their phones."

The room got even colder when I heard that, so cold that I wrapped my arms around my shoulders and rubbed them to warm myself. "I-I never spent the night with an ERA before."

"First time for everything, fresh meat."

Gwen skipped over to me and draped an arm over my shoulder. Her auburn brown hair was a complete contrast to her extremely fair complexion, even in the dim lighting of the club. "Yes! I can finally have a meal with someone who'll appreciate it."

Hearing Rana chuckle, I watched as Ebony walked over to us and sucked her teeth. "I'll appreciate you not burning whatever mess you try to make tonight."

"That happened one time! When you gonna let it go?"

"I'll let it go when you pay for the damages your little stir fry disaster cost me."

I felt Gwen's arm slip down from my shoulder and almost swallowed my tongue when she playfully poked Ebony's chest. "Why everything have to come down to money with you?"

"Seeing as I'mma be around for a while, ain't no sense in being broke."

The two of them laughed and made their way to the back entrance. I found myself watching Wilma as she went over to Rana at the bar.

I mean, if I'm going to be sleeping under an ERA's roof, I would rather it be the one that made me feel safe, right?

Just as I was about to ask if I could crash at Wilma's place instead, Gwen turned back to look at me with a small smile on her face.

"C'mon Jael. I'll cook something extra special to welcome you home."

I don't know if it was the promise of a home cooked meal, or the way Gwen's eyes lit up as she looked at me. But whatever it was had me walking to join them.

Rules

IT HAD BEEN A MONTH since I moved in with Ebony and Gwen, and I can't lie - it feels good as hell to sleep in a real bed again.

I even got an upgrade from 'fresh meat' to 'cheeky' from Ebony, which all the other girls told me was a good thing.

"You should make it your stage name." Keki suggested while we were getting dressed for work that night.

Tam nodded in agreement as she laced up her heels. "Hell yeah! Them ERAs will eat that up."

"Better that than me." I muttered.

All the new girls that made it past the first month now could dance privately for everyone, and that included ERAs. To say I was nervous as fuck would've been an understatement. I know they tipped well - hell Keki counted out almost three stacks after giving Ebony her cut last night. But still...the way they moved in silence like ninjas and sipped spiked donor shots from the bar left me feeling some type of way.

Lost in my thoughts, I didn't notice when Tam stood behind me until she placed her chin in the crook of my neck. Staring at our reflections together in the floor-length mirror, my eyes widened as I saw Wilma watching. Tam reached out and brushed her soft hands along the white fishnet dress I wore over my neon green floss. When my breath hitched, she giggled.

"I can think of one ERA that wouldn't mind eating you up," Tam whispered in my ear. "Maybe you should let her."

Tam placed a quick kiss on my cheek and as she strolled away, I glanced in the mirror again and found Wilma still there.

Over the last month, we've spent some time together outside of work. At first, I thought she was just being nice, since the night they all found out that those dudes had my info. Before I left Smackz, Ebony told me to sell my car to a junkyard as soon as possible.

That next day, Wilma drove in her truck behind me and helped me take out my belongings before accepting eight bills for the car I'd had since high school. During that time, I really came to look forward to seeing Wilma. From our grocery runs and late night chats into the early morning on the bed of her truck, Wilma was a vibe that I wanted to be around all the time. But could I really, you know, be her girl? Like that?

I brought in my bottom lip and watched Wilma close her eyes. She let one of those rare small smiles grace her face. I could feel the heat rise in my cheeks, and when my heart sped up, Wilma's fangs were on full display in the mirror. My eyes grew, but I didn't move - I couldn't.

I don't know if it was because it was the first time I'd seen her fangs, or if it was the fact that I wasn't nervous about seeing them. My hands went up to my warm cheeks, and I tried to keep the corner of my lips from turning upward as I stared at her. Just like that, my mind was made up, and I closed my eyes in acceptance. When I opened them, my reflection was all I saw in the mirror. That was until Keki rushed past me and smacked my ass.

"Let's go turn it out!"

"You play too much!" I called out to her while following her to the main floor.

* * *

It was definitely the weekend, because Smackz was packed!

ERAs and regular folks were lined up around every stage, waiting for someone to get out of their seat. Even the private dance spaces between the wall and stages were full. I watched on as Tam and a new girl tagged team one dude, who was smiling like he'd won the lotto.

Before my turn on the pole, I was scheduled to be at the door. Keki waved as she took her place beside Gwen behind the bar. On my way to the curtain that separated the entrance from the main floor, Gwen jogged toward me. "Hey, you decided on your official stage name? I gotta let the DJ know before your set."

I thought back to what Tam said to me in the dressing room and answered. "Yeah. Tell 'em I go by 'Cheeks'"

Gwen's giggle broke out through the music and I joined her. "Ebony's gonna love that."

I went to the podium and waited for the girl taking a payment to finish before I took over. With no one in line to get inside, I looked up at the large purple neon clock and tried to keep my breathing steady when I noticed Wilma switch off with Di, the new ERA added to security, in the 'magician slip' behind me. We called the space that separated the girls at the front from the security on duty the magician slip because with the two meters of curtain space that separated us, it looked like I was alone to anyone that came in from outside. But I knew for sure Wilma was there when I could smell the mint and rosemary fragrance that she liked to wear.

My heart was racing when I counted the drawer, and I knew Wilma heard it, even as I finally spoke. "Hey."

"How you doing, Jael?"

Other than Gwen, no one else used my real name, and knowing that made the butterflies in my stomach take flight. Putting away the bills, I sanitized my hands and waved them around to dry. Once I sat down in the tall black swivel chair, I crossed my legs and ignored the rapid tapping sound that my heels made.

"I'm good. But...um, I was wondering..." Clearing my throat, I tried again, "You wanna see a movie at the new drive-in sometime?"

"W-with you?"

"Yeah. You know, after our next trip to the grocery store? We can catch one of those late night showings. And...talk."

"Oh, yeah. I'm down for that."

"Okay."

Wilma's chuckle was low, but just hearing it made my ears heat up. The front door swung open, and I tried not to frown as I spotted Kitty strut up to the podium with two dudes on either side. Her mid length dress clung to her petite frame, with circle cutouts on the sides that showed off her waist. When she finally looked up at me and rolled her eyes, I gripped the edge of the podium while standing up.

"I can't believe you made it this long here." Kitty murmured. "I guess it really do be the quiet ones, uh?"

Ignoring her remarks and getting straight to it, I said directly, "It's $250 for entrance."

"How much?!" one guy demanded, as he jerked his head back in disbelief.

"Men's entrance fee is $100 each. Women and enbies are $50. So y'alls total is $250."

Kitty reached into her cleavage and pulled out a small stack. She peeled off three bills and tossed them onto the podium. I bit the inside of my jaw as I took the money and placed it into the register. Though before I could give Kitty the change, she thrust a hand in the air. "You can 'gone head and keep that change. Just give us the wristbands."

I put the extra money inside the tip jar on the counter before placing a wristband on each of their wrists. The last guy licked his lips when I tugged on the ends of his band.

"When you taking the stage?" he drawled out while ogling my chest.

"I ain't on the floor tonight." I lied. "Just working the door."

Kitty tsked while looking me up and down. "That's too bad, would've loved to see what you can do."

Once they walked past me to enter the main room, Wilma stepped out from behind the magical slip to pat each one of them down. I sighed as the three of them entered the club.

"You good, Jael? I can get another girl to cover for you for a minute."

"I'm good, thanks." I whispered. "But can you please make sure everyone knows who just came in?"

"Already did. Boss gave us the green light to toss 'em out the second they breathe wrong."

The thought of Kitty and her entourage getting thrown out brought a smile to my face. And as the music changed from a southern trap classic to a more hip hop tempo, I just knew I was gonna see that happen when I heard Kitty's voice again.

"Girl, no! Who taught you how to twerk?!"

Not wanting to miss the action, I took the rope that hung on a nail in the wall and tied it around one side of the curtain. The guys were already standing at the stage furthest from the entrance, so I looked over at the bar and saw Keki talking with a customer. Even though she was talking to them, her eyes drifted away toward Kitty every few seconds. Someone got up from their chair at the main stage, and Kitty wasted no time claiming it. Leaning back, she propped her heels across the small railing and smirked at everyone near the stage.

Within a minute, I saw Gwen march over to Kitty, and for a second I almost didn't recognize her. Gone was the cheery smile I'd gotten used to seeing, and a steel glare was in its place.

"You came to take notes? Or to find out when our next amature night is?"

"Ah, Becky the comedian. Should've known you'd be here."

"And you 'bout to be on your way out. Hope you enjoyed yourself."

Kitty looked up at Gwen and frowned. "Just cause you sound a little Black, don't mean shit, withcha lily white ass."

"That's what you came all this way to say to me?" Gwen scoffed before adding, "And in ya 'lil prom dress too?"

"You know what - I'm gettin' real sick of your mouth, bitch!"

Several patrons slowly got up and went to the other side of the stage. Kitty moved her feet from the railing and planted them on the floor. Everyone else stopped pretending not to stare when Gwen towered over Kitty.

"And I'm sick of seein' your ass all together. You know where the exit is - bitch."

"I ain't going nowhere."

"That's just what I wanted to hear." Gwen grinned as Di appeared by her side. "Let me personally see you out then."

"I thought you said you was gonna try to get rid of me by yourself?"

"I am. Di's here to make sure I don't fuck you all the way up."

The last thing I saw before the lights went out was Kitty's fist sailing toward Gwen's face. Seconds after the lights went out, the front doors burst open. Several figures in all black were at the entrance, holding both doors wide open. I screamed when I felt a pair of arms grab my waist, but soon the smell of rosemary and mint calmed me down. Wilma's voice was low. "Stay down and outta sight."

She didn't wait for a response as she rushed out from behind the curtain, immediately making contact with one of the figures. I briefly saw Wilma fang out as she fought hand to hand with them. My breathing was heavy as I heard the sounds of grunts and shouts around me. A loud banging sound close by made me bring my knees close to my chest.

"Take the cash and find Kitty!"

"Told y'all not to bring her on for this!"

The emergency lights finally came on, and my eyes adjusted to the change as I listened to the guys out front raid the cash register. Through the small opening of the curtain, I watched as more Smackz security showed up. They were dodging chains that a few of the guys whipped through the air. Smoke made its way to my nose, and I placed a hand over my mouth when bright flames raced up the curtains in front of me. A gust of wind brushed against my feet, and my heart threatened to give out at the sight of Wilma in front of me, her white long-sleeved shirt covered in blood.

I said nothing as she scooped me up. Instinctively, I wrapped my arms around Wilma's neck and tightly shut my eyes. The absence of her solid chest was immediate, and I blinked as she disappeared again. In front of me was Keki and two other girls, each of us staring wide eyed at one another as we hid on the floor inside the bar area. When I started to speak, the girl closest to Keki held up her index finger and quickly shook her head. Nodding, I remained quiet and grabbed Keki's hand.

The sound of slaps and punches echoed around us, and I could feel Keki's hold on me tighten. Soon there were growls and screams that followed, before Gwen's voice roared out, "Ebony - DOWN!"

Metal clanked against metal, and Ebony's cries filled the club.

"Keep the chains on her!" one dude grunted out. "I'll douse more gas and light her up."

My legs shook, but I refused to leave the spot where Wilma left me, no matter how bad I wanted to see what was going on.

"You ain't all tough now, is you?"

Kitty's voice taunted everyone in earshot, but I knew it was Ebony that she was talking to once she spoke again. "How does it feel to be the one dangling in the air, taking a beating in front of your friends?"

One of the girls' heels touched mine, and I snapped my head toward her. With a shaking hand, she lifted her index finger, and I followed the movement. Above us were three panel mirrors that gave us a view of the main stage, allowing us to see what was happening. Soft gurgling sounds were all that I heard before Kitty's dark laughter.

"Yeah, I'm gonna enjoy this shit. Give me that damn flare gun."

"No! Boss said to send a message. That's it!"

"Fuck that! She finna die twice!" Kitty shouted.

"No...she ain't, bitch."

A spark of neon red flew toward Kitty, and soon her screams ricocheted off the walls. I brought my hand over my mouth to keep from throwing up at the sickly, sweet, sulfur like smell that filled the air as Kitty fell to the floor. In the mirror above, we saw Gwen holding her chest as she slowly stood. Security had the drop on the last dudes that rushed the club, but Gwen's attention was on Kitty's burning body as she dragged her feet toward her.

Ebony wasn't too far away and my eyes widened as I watched her sank her fangs into a guy's chest. His body twitched while Ebony pressed her hand down on his chest, greedily taking in his blood. Half the burns and scars she got from the fire and the chains that they'd used to pin her down were almost gone. But she didn't stop feeding until Gwen took a step closer to Kitty.

Ebony's eyes dilated when she dropped the body in front of her back to the ground. My eyes blinked twice from trying to keep up with the speed Ebony used to reach Gwen. The flare gun dropped from Gwen's hand, and she collapsed forward. Ebony caught her before she landed on top of Kitty, who managed to lift up her chin from the ground.

"We...still got ya ass." Kitty wheezed out. "Bitch."

Seeing the baseball sized hole at the back of her neck, Kitty briefly reminded me of a plastic doll that was tossed into a flaming grill. Where her neck met her spine, she was completely covered in not only blood, but also burns. The mid shoulder length bundles Kitty pranced into the club with earlier had caught fire and singed, plastering to the side of her face.

When one of the girls behind the bar stood, the rest of us did the same. We huddled around the front of the bar and watched as Ebony shouted while tearing and clawing at Gwen's blood soaked dress, "Gwen! W-where is the wound?" When she didn't answer Ebony quick enough, she shook Gwen. "Talk to me! Where is it?"

Gwen's hand fell, exposing a large gash on her chest. Blood spurted from her lips as she coughed, and red tears filled Ebony's eyes. The two stared at one another before Ebony brushed the tears away. I could hear the strain in Ebony's voice when she spoke.

"You know we pro-choice 'round here, so what's it gonna be?"

Gwen's voice was hoarse as she stared up at Ebony. "Can you...send my mama my stacks? Th-they at the house...in the pink cr-crockpot you bought me."

"Gwen...are you sure? Cause I-"

Gwen ignored Ebony's question as her eyes traveled over to the bar. "Make sure she gets the letters in my locker too. 81-09-11."

"Okay."

I heard someone sniffle and turned my head to see Keki's eyes full of tears. I was on the verge of crying too, but I couldn't. The one thing on my mind was saving Gwen. Just watching everyone around me acting like this was normal left my body shaking. Keki tried to put a hand around my waist, and I shook it away. Taking a step toward Gwen and Ebony, I felt the air change as Di soon stood in the way. My entire body felt like it was on fire as I was forced to watch Gwen and not do anything.

"Somebody get me... get me a shot of tequila." Gwen requested weakly.

Wilma's voice was heavy as she answered. "Bet."

She blew past us to the bar and was in front of Gwen before I turned to look back at Di, who now stood next to me. With a shaky hand, Gwen accepted the drink and put it to her lips. Taking a small sip, they all looked on while the small glass fell to the ground, its remaining contents trickling toward Kitty's lifeless body. "Shit...that was Tres Mujeres too..."

Ebony took Gwen's limp hand into hers, brushing her cheek along the pale knuckles. "It's okay. Just let me try -" She turned her head away for a second before snapping it back to face Gwen's. "Yeah, it was. You was the one that told me to stop serving basic booze up in here."

They shared another giggle, but I could only see a faint smile on Gwen's face. In that moment, I was glad she scorched Kitty's ass. For taking away the most beautiful sound I'd heard in years - if Gwen hadn't ended Kitty, in that second I would have.

"Out of all the bosses I had, yo...you was the best."

I couldn't stomach hearing Ebony chuckle, but with Di brushing up against my left arm, all I could do was lower my head as I pressed my lips tighter together. Seeing Gwen like this and Ebony doing nothing was gonna get me killed.

I tried not to get close to anyone when I started here, but that girl was hard to shake. Tears burned my eyes as I watched my friend cough and Ebony wiped away the blood that spilled from Gwen's lips.

"I done heard some scary shit in my life, but that is fo 'sho the scariest."

Ebony's lackluster laughter blended in with the sniffles around me and I bit down hard on my bottom lip. I didn't bother trying to brush away Di's cool hand when she brought it around my waist.

"You always had my back Ebony, ever since high school. And...you gave me a-a chance to do more than just survive this fucked up town."

"We had each other's back, Gwen."

"You more than m-mine. Than-."

Gwen's body started convulsing before she went completely still. Her eyes were wide as her head stared upward. Ebony pressed her face into Gwen's chest while all the other girls around me silently cried. We watched as Ebony closed Gwen's eyes, gently laying her head on the ground before standing.

Ebony just drained a dude and didn't have so much as a scratch on her. She could have saved Gwen - I just know it. So why didn't she?

"Di, call the cleaning crew." Ebony whispered after a minute of silence.

Seeing Di take a phone out of the back pocket of her cargo pants, my rage took over as I finally shouted at Ebony, "You're an ERA! Why you ain't save her?"

Tears left my eyes and I didn't bother brushing them away. If Ebony took me out for getting loud with her, she for damn sure was gonna see why.

Ebony paused and turned her head halfway toward me. I could see her pause as she stared down at Gwen's face before moving at super speed to the far end of the club. When Ebony went through the backdoor, I looked up and saw Rana right next to me. She looked so tiny next to me in my clear platform heels that if I hadn't seen her toss two dudes twice her size earlier, I would've had no idea she was an ERA. Her hand touched mine, and it was warm. Gwen told me once that ERAs weren't always cold, like most vamp stories said and I didn't believe her. As Rana led me to the chairs in front of the main stage, I felt more tears build in my eyes as I thought about telling Gwen she was right and immediately remembering that I can't.

Rana waited for me to sit in the chair next to her before speaking. "Before you got here, what did you hear about us?"

"What that got to do with anything?"

"It matters. So please answer the question."

Rana let go of my hand and looked at me for a minute before I did what she asked.

"On the news, they said the same thing - stay away, y'all dangerous. But my friend Amanda had a friend who went to get the vaccine and came back an ERA. For a week, we hung out with her friend and didn't know until Amanda's boyfriend came out running one day, shouting for us to get away from them."

I saw one of Rana's hands grip the railing and heard it squeak. When she let the railing go, it looked like a crushed soda can.

"That's it?" Rana asked.

"Yeah."

"So you never seen or heard what happens to someone after they're bitten?"

"I told you I don't know!" I groaned. "What does that have to do with Ebony letting Gwen die like that?"

Rana closed her eyes, and I felt the coolness of her breath when it ghosted across my face. She scrunched up her eyes and quickly shook her head before opening them to look at me again. Her glare didn't scare me, as I met it with one of my own.

"Since we came back from the dead, some of us have tried to turn others with a bite. And the results, well, they are almost worse than death."

Curious, I asked, "What do you mean?"

"Black and brown folks were involved in those vaccine tests, and so far, the majority of those that returned afterwards have been women. A few men, but they ain't as enhanced as the women are, which is one reason why Smackz has an all-female security team."

Rana let out a chuckle that I knew wasn't meant to be funny from how she cut her eyes to the main entrance before returning her stare back to me. "Before I started working here, a few male ERAs I heard about in passing were trying to grow a following. They were big mad that women like us had power in dying that they didn't." Rana released a deep sigh, and I listened closely when she continued.

"It was worse than any gang war I'd seen. Bodies on top of bodies in run-down houses - no survivors. Only decaying bodies." Rana paused, and I watched as she took a deep breath. "Since all this was happening in the ghetto, the law ain't care, so the bodies kept piling up. Folks finally wised up and stopped going out there, but some of the male ERAs that were a part of the new group that were trying to turn people broke rank after not getting fed regularly."

Rana looked past me, toward the bar, and sighed before she went on. "Some tried to return back to live with non-ERAs, but people were rightfully scared of them. They were hunted down and ran out of town. The male ERAs that somehow remained from that following...they were so desperate to feed that they'd go inside to find the freshest body they could. The folks that saw them from far away said they looked like junkies - sniffing around for a hit off of a discarded pipe."

I shuddered. "You said that only folks like us were in these places. What about, you know?"

I looked over to where I last saw Gwen and turned back to Rana. Her eyes were bloodshot red as she whispered, "My partner, Tyler, was against me going to the medical center, but I needed money for tuition. When I came back home, he was so damn happy. And he begged me to..."

As her voice trailed off, I watched Rana wipe the red tears away from her face and said nothing. "After I bit him, it was like watching a ticking bomb. Boils showed up all over his body. Tyler screamed and soiled himself before his body liquified."

"Liquified?" I repeated softly.

"From what I could find online about others that were non-melanated and bitten by an ERA, it's what happens when your insides burn at inhuman temperatures. In Tyler's case, it started with his eyes. They were the first of his organs to go."

I couldn't imagine having to see someone I cared about suffer through that. Remembering the last words I heard Ebony say to Gwen, it sounded like she was willing to take that chance.

"So far, not one white person to date has survived a bite from an ERA." Rana told me while staring off at the main stage. "Gwen knew this and made her choice."

We sat in silence for a moment, and I took in everything Rana told me. Her soft voice soon interrupted my thoughts. "Ebony may not always show it, but she does care about the girls that work here. For her to have to put down Gwen that way... I wouldn't wish that on nobody."

I watched as Rana finally stood and walked away. Soon I was thinking about everything she'd just shared with me, my friendships with the other girls at the club, and whatever was going on between me and Wilma. The scent of rust and stale smoke followed me when I got up from the chair and went to the changing room. Looking in the mirror, I stared at my reflection and made a vow to myself out loud.

"Just one more month. One more month and I'll leave."

THE NEW BEGINNING

The way this new beginning set up...
Revolution - Maya
Reunited - Kem
Rebirth - Kem

Revolution, part one

Maya

A WHOLE YEAR LATER, and I still can't believe how different my life is right now. Went from waiting on the bus with my girls for school to waiting for the sun to drop low enough for me to actually enjoy being outside without irritating my skin for a few hours. I low key missed those days. At least I was with my girls. Now I'm all alone and wishing I hadn't talked them into skipping school to take that stupid vaccine with me.

With the sun disappearing from the sky, I took off the oversize hoodie and tied it around my waist. People walked past me and I kept my head down, making sure to not catch their stares. Even as the girl closest to me sucked in her teeth, I kept moving and focused on the fresh smell of clean meat before it sizzled onto something hot, probably a grill.

"Aye! Aye! Y'all look over there!"

I tried not to look up, but when the stomping of feet behind me grew louder and louder, I whipped my head up to see a red and white building with the name 'Hot Wings and Thangs' painted in orange script over a large farm red door. A woman wearing an apron with a big gap tooth smile was painted on the side of the building. Several long wooden benches were out front, covered by red and white checkered plastic.

I heard the small creaking sound as the door on the side of the building open. Immediately, I crouched low and scanned my eyes for a clear exit. Though before I could sprint away, a tall man in denim shorts, a white shirt, and long white ribbed socks with checkered sliders wandered out the same door and glanced across the street. I got a better view of his face when he tilted his head up over the green trucker hat he wore. The small patches of gray hair along his jaw didn't match the twinkle found in his warm brown eyes. He looked old enough to be my granddad, holding a pair of tongs and a big metal bowl as he called out to the crowd, "Y'all hungry? Bout to put some links and thangs out. If ya want some, they on the house today."

A few people around me whispered in hushed voices, and the man let out a chuckle. "Well, I hope y'all find your voices by the time it's done."

Two little girls skipped out from inside the brick building, all smiles. They couldn't have been no more than eight or nine years old, each with their hair in plaits and colorful barrettes on the ends. Their pink and orange dresses twirled around them as they moved around the benches. The girl in the orange dress reached out and poked the other before they both came to a stop and giggled.

The sight of them instantly sent my mind to the day before me and my girls went to get the vaccine. Flashes of us at the mall, laughing at the boys that tried to holla at us and trying on ugly dresses filled my thoughts. To keep myself from falling down memory lane, I made a beeline across the street toward the restaurant, making sure to sit at the bench furthest away from everyone else.

When I finished taking in all the people that had either decided to keep away or sit and wait for a plate, I felt eyes behind me. Bringing in my shoulders, I slowly turned my head to the left. The two little girls from earlier stared at me, and I tried to hurry up and untie my hoodie to hide some of the scars on my wrists from them.

"Tracey! Tonya! Leave that girl alone!"

The three of us jumped from the booming voice. I watched as the man from before made his way over to me, this time with a woman by his side as the two girls grinned up at him.

One of them looked back at me and said, "Daddy! We just wanted to say hey."

"Uh hmm, gone and tell another lie," he teased, winking at the woman beside him as she smiled at the girls.

"We was!" the other one said, before whispering loudly toward the woman, "I think she's like you, auntie."

My eyes widened as the woman looked at me. When she met my stare and nodded, the girl in the orange continued. "I told you Tonya! She a E-R-Ah."

I tried to focus on the sleeves of my hoodie, but I could still feel them staring at me. Taking a deep breath, I peered over at the woman, dressed in jeans and a long sleeve tee. Her light purple head wrap added six inches to her height, making her half a foot shorter than the older man in front of her. She kissed both the girls and then the man before looking back at me.

"Willie, let me talk to your guest right quick, okay?"

When she sat down on the far end of the bench, I tried not to stare. If I hadn't heard their conversation a minute ago, I wouldn't have believed for a second that she was an ERA. The woman in front of me looked like everyone I steered clear of. Her deep bronze skin ain't have one blemish on it, and when she flashed her pearly white teeth my way, I didn't think for a second that she would cause me harm.

She looked too normal to be a useless monster like me.

"What's your name?"

Even her voice was soft, like a lullaby. I couldn't meet her stare as I whispered, "Maya."

"It's good to see you, Maya."

I wanted to believe her words so bad. So much so that I mustered up the courage to look at her head on. Her smile grew, and for the first time in months, I felt something I ain't think I would again. My eyes started to burn, and as quick as lightning, she disappeared.

Before I could wonder where she went, she was standing right in front of me, holding a red plastic cup and what looked like a small package. This time, when she sat down, it was directly across from me. She sat the cup down in front of me and I bit back a groan. Slowly, I reached out for the cup and almost sighed as the warmth from inside it touched my hands.

"It look like it's been some time since you fed."

My stomach lurched forward, and I gripped the cup tightly as I raised it to my lips. Once the heady flavor made it onto my tongue, I greedily gulped down the rest of its contents.

"You feel better?"

When I shook my head yes, she let out a small laugh. "I know we can still eat, but it ain't the same."

With the red cup back on the wooden table, I stared between it and her. "Nah, not at all."

I thought of the meals I forced myself to eat over the last year and sighed, "It's like...a memory now." I tried to explain, "Like, the food is real, but I'm trying to eat a memory of what it used to taste like to me."

"That's a good way to describe it."

Willie walked out of the side door again, this time carrying enough food to leave a basketball team with the itis. Another memory jumbled around in my mind of my brothers all rushing to the kitchen after mama and me cooked Sunday dinner. Then just as quick, I remembered the long walk home with Gia after waking up and leaving the vaccine clinic. When I saw their faces as they recognized what I'd become...

I closed my eyes while turning my head from the rest of that thought as everyone around me cheered. The woman's hand on top of mine was soft as her voice, and for a minute it felt warm when she spoke. "How long have you been on your own out there?"

"A few months now. Ever since my girl Gia got lit up."

"Lit up?" she asked.

This time I couldn't stop the tears from rushing to my eyes. Meeting her stare, I took a deep breath and let it out. "Yeah. You heard of the Sons of Light? The ERA hunters group?"

When she nodded, I forced myself to go on. "We were hiding out with some other peeps one night when we heard them outside the building. They tried to trap us inside while they torched it."

I could almost feel the heat from being locked in that old comic book shop on my skin. To shake it off, I brought my hands to my sides and rubbed them. Her eyes never left mine as I spoke again.

"Me and my homegirl Gia managed to get out through a window. Those screams..." Clearing my throat, I shut my eyes, like it would help me not relieve everything that happened. "But when we took off running, a group of hunters caught Gia with a black cord. It looked like an electrical whip or something. I tried - I tried to get it from around her neck, but all I did was get myself burned."

My hands went in search of the sleeves of my hoodie as I tried to cover up the scars on my fingers and wrists.

I could cover the scars, but the sizzling and pop from the cord around Gia's neck, and the screams that ripped through my friend's mouth just seconds before she told me to run will never leave my mind. Seeing her face twist with pain as the whip around her throat tightened, I was forced to watch my friend use her last breath to tell me to save myself. I didn't realize that I drew blood from curling my fists together until I felt the wetness seep through the thin tank top I was wearing.

"You ain't gotta tell me anymore if you don't want to."

I knew that, but I wanted to tell her. Someone needed to know what happened. And even though I wasn't able to save Gia, I needed to tell someone about her. Gia was the only one out of our crew - other than me - to make it out of that place. And one day, if I could, I wanted to make Sons of Light pay for what they did.

"Weeks after Gia was lit up, I saw a video that those bastards recorded. They had chained her and several other ERAs to the front of massive trucks and ..." Tears fell down my face as I closed them in an attempt to rid myself of the images that followed.

The woman in front of me pushed the small package from earlier closer, and I saw that it was a pack of hand wipes. She removed the card that was on top and peeled the seal before taking out a wipe and handing it to me. "I'm so sorry they did that to you and your friend."

Everyone around us was eating and talking, even Tonya and Tracey. A little boy soon joined them and the three of them started playing a game of tag as Willie watched on from the grill. They all looked so happy, free of any problems. I was jealous just watching them enjoy life, when mines had been forever changed. As I got lost in my thoughts, I felt a hand gently squeeze mine.

"I put together a few safe houses for folks like us. You're welcome to visit the one here in town. The address is on this card."

"For real? What do I have to do when I get there?"

She blinked a few times before a soft smile graced her face. "Baby girl, you ain't got to do anything. And you can stay as long as you like while deciding what you want to do next."

My eyes widened as I saw the truth in her words. Tonya, Tracey, and their new friend sprinted over to us. The little boy reached us first, extending his tiny arms toward the woman and smiling at her.

"What's your name?" I asked, as she slowly stood up.

Instead of answering, the woman scooped up the small boy in her arms and he giggled before placing a kiss on her cheek.

"You be sure to come to the address on that card tomorrow, okay?"

"O-okay."

I picked up the card as she walked away and bit my lip. She seemed for real, but what about the other people that were gonna be there? Would they be as cool welcoming another person into their place?

I didn't know for sure, but since I ain't have nowhere else to go, I stuffed the card and wipes into the side pockets of my jeans. With my hoodie back on, I slowly made my way from the benches, but not before glancing back one last time. Seeing the woman at the grill with Willie, I watched as they both laughed.

I could at least see about the place on the card - from a distance. And if it didn't feel right, I'd leave. So that's what I decided to do.

    * * *

Finding the building didn't even take me that long. Once I got settled inside a small abandoned shop down the street, I watched the green two-story apartment complex from a smashed window. There wasn't a name on it, but I guess they didn't need one, since there was always someone there. People came and went from the complex, from mamas with their kids to ladies old enough to be my granny - even as the sun went down. They all looked normal, until an hour after sunset. That was when I noticed more women showing up, dressed in camouflage and boots - some of them wore thick neon red biker jackets.

What stood out about them wasn't just their vibe, but a symbol. It looked like half of a wreath, the ones people hung on their doors during Christmas time. But just above it was a single sword and a small tear. Everyone that showed up after the sunset had that symbol on them somehow. Either as a tattoo or as a gold pendant. I even peeped the sister that had the symbol etched onto both sides of her fade while she talked to another chick as they stood on the roof of the apartment building.

She wore a mini yet wild mohawk, with braids on the side of it. For a second I thought she could see me watching them, but I knew that wasn't possible.

There were still ordinary looking folks that walked into the complex. They would stop and say hey to the people wearing the symbol before disappearing inside their homes. It seemed like a safe enough place so far, but that don't mean I'll like it. Though as I looked around the dusty and empty shop, I knew I had to at least give it a shot. After another hour of watching the complex, I got bored and called it a night.

Morning came, and I used the last of the wipes from the barbeque joint to try to clean myself up before leaving. There was a thick overcast, so I chose to wrap my hoodie around my waist as I walked along the sidewalk. When I arrived at the building, birds chirped above my head as the street and foot traffic picked up. All the chatter on the sidewalk and honking horns almost made me catch whiplash from looking around at each new sound. Finally, I stood in front of the green apartment complex and reached into the pocket of my jeans. Taking out the business card from yesterday, I looked to see if there was anything on the back that would tell me what to do once I got there.

"You Maya?"

My shoulders tightened before I turned around. A woman the same height as me, with a more muscular build step toward me, but when I started to turn to go in the opposite direction, she paused.

"Mother said you'd be by today. I'm Pearl." she said.

I tilted my head, curiosity taking over. "Whose Mother?"

Pearl smiled before answering, "The sista you met at Willie's yesterday? That's what we call her, Mother."

I never did get her name, and hearing Pearl give me one that made sense got me to lower my shoulders as I faced her.

"Oh. Yeah, okay."

"We're glad you're here at The Garden."

Before Pearl could answer, three more women appeared behind me. I recognized the tallest one first, with the braids and mohawk. She smirked at me and I immediately took two steps back.

"Be nice Luna. Maya is new to The Garden."

I stared at Luna before asking, "The Garden?"

"What? You didn't see the sign while you were staking us out last night?" Luna said.

Her words repeated in my head and just as I figured out what she meant, the others giggled.

"H-how did you know that? I was three blocks away!"

The woman next to Luna leaned closer to me and I tried not to poke my lip out, which only seemed to make them laugh more.

"She cute." One woman mused before introducing herself. "I'm Viv. This is my wife Max and her sister Andrea." Seeing her still try not to laugh made me want to leave, but I couldn't without first walking past them.

Max waved while flashing a grin. "It's nice to meet you Maya. We hope you'll stay."

Luna smirked as she looked me up and down. "Yeah, you should stay. At least until you learn how to really stake out a place." She said, reaching out and patting me on the head.

"Don't let Luna get to you," Viv told me. "She ain't know much when she got here either."

Luna sucked her teeth as the others laughed. Pearl walked over to me and met my stare. She was definitely older than me, but I wasn't sure by how much. Guess it don't matter if she's an ERA, since we can live forever. As the thought ran through my mind, a laugh slipped out of my lips. The surrounding woman didn't ask why, instead they joined me. And I don't know why sharing a laugh with them made me feel better, but it did.

"We're about to set up for our monthly dinner." Pearl said. "This one is kind of a big deal, so we'd love it if you stayed."

"But, don't y'all feel weird?" I found myself asking. "Eating food in front of folks?"

Andrea was the first to answer, "Everyone here feeds before the non ERAs do."

"The better for us to patrol while partying." Luna sing songed as she skipped over between Viv and Max.

I watched as the three of them walked off without saying a word and with Luna gone, I had one more question. "What can I do to help?"

* * *

After helping Pearl and the others bring out over a dozen long tables, chairs, and food, I sat down at the end of one of the tables outside. A few kids passed by and stopped to sit on the large generator. One of them took out a small boombox. Watching them dance and tease each other while listening to the radio, more memories of time with my girls came back to me. Though this time I didn't look away. With the sun beaming down on me, I could feel a smile spread across my face.

"Hey, you okay?"

I turned to face Pearl and answered softly, "I think so."

The music ended and more kids crowded the generator as a voice came over the boombox.

"Y'all know who it is - the Manpower Rush Hour coming to ya! And today we have a new guest, one of the few realest to have survived the DELTA X vaccines. Gone 'head and tell the people who you is bruh."

"Yeah, yeah, call me Rizen."

"Oh, word?"

"Yeah. See, see, my government name was Christopher Browning, but after being reborn, I freed myself of that life and now live with my four wives as the Rizen King."

One boy in the group outside sucked his teeth, "My daddy say one wife is hard enough to keep happy and this dude say he got fo?"

"Man, he cappin'!"

As the kids laughed, I continued to listen.

"So tell us why you finally agreed to come in the studio, Rizen?"

Before Rizen spoke, another guy interrupted. "Probably had to get permission from all his females."

"Nah brother. See-see-see, the reason I came here is to spread the word for those like you who are blinded to the truth. Today is the celebration of my rebirth."

"That's right. It's been a year since the vaccine incident."

"That's right. And I'm here to spread the word with those that want to bring an end to the reign that these loose and vile women have had over us."

"Oh word? Just what you and your wives gonna do about them ERA bitches? Word on the street is you can't even hold your own one on one with 'em."

The other dudes chuckled before Rizen spoke again. "Me and my fellow resurrected kings have reached out to a group that calls themselves the Sons of Light. And with their help, we will be putting an end to the reign of all ERAs that refuse to acknowledge us true kings. For too long they have turned away from the true order of things and we will make them see the light."

I stood up and narrowed my eyes at the boombox.

"Oh, so since you can't fight 'em head up, you went and got reinforcements?"

"Tonight, we will make our presence known throughout the city, and those that try to step in will be swiftly handled. The Sons of Light an-"

"Y'all turn that mess off." An older woman called out to the kids from a window.

I wanted to hear what else them fools on the radio had to say. Anything that had something to do with Sons of Light was hot news for me, and if they were still in town I wanted to know where. Because I was done running.

I was ready for revenge.

As the kids did what they were told, another voice cut through the crowd.

"I see you made it baby girl."

The rage I felt made it hard for me to turn around to the sound of Mother's voice. It was calming and clear, just like it was yesterday, but I didn't want to hear it. Today she wore all blue in different shades, from the dark blue head wrap, long sleeve sky blue blouse, and acid-washed jeans. Her smile as she made her way toward me was still the same, just as warm and inviting as it was yesterday. I didn't realize my fists were curled up until I saw her eyes sweep downward and I followed.

"You okay Maya?"

Luna and Max were on either side of Mother, both grinning up at her before Max answered for me.

"I think Luna hurt her feelings."

Luna sided eyed Max before turning her attention to Mother. "I was just being honest Mother. She really thought she had the drop on us!"

Mother reached out and swatted at Luna's shoulder. "You ain't have to say nothing, Lunie."

The way Luna was cheesing, you would've thought Mother just called her the first female president of the United States. Mother closed the distance between us, wrapping me into her arms. I almost lost my train of thought as she rocked me from side to side. Just as I closed my eyes, she released her hold on me.

"I'm sure you know by now what we're celebrating tonight, right?"

Come to think of it, I didn't know. Yeah, Pearl told me that this monthly dinner was special, but after that, we spent the rest of our time setting everything up. Mother and Max looked at one another and shared a knowing glance. Though when she stared at me, I didn't feel any judgment from her for not having an answer. Instead, Mother brought a hand to my cheek as she told me gently, "We're celebrating our first birthdays."

With a quick wink, Mother kissed my cheek and smirked. "Happy birthday Maya."

Revolution, part two

IT'D BEEN A MINUTE since I been to a party. Though most of the parties I went to were either a block party or somebody trying to get the rent money mixers. Andrea passed out red plastic cups to all us ERAs and collected them just as quick once we gulped down the lukewarm blood inside. Before I knew it, a group of dudes had opened the windows to an apartment on the first floor and filled each one with subwoofer speakers.

The kids from earlier had come back down and started playing a mean game of four square. Seeing them jumping around in their concrete corners and talking trash to one another, I could've sworn I felt my heart beat. My eyes stung when more memories rushed to the surface. Just when I was about to bring my hand out to wipe the tears away, a small red towel flashed in front of my face.

"I got you." Max said.

I looked up at her and accepted the towel. "Thanks."

Cheers erupted around us and I looked over in time to see two kids switching spots as another dribbled the basketball on the hard concrete.

Max nudged me before asking, "You must've had a little brother in your old life."

I didn't answer her right away, taking a second to force down the ragged lump lodged in my throat. "Nah. I was the little sister."

"Oh, my bad. Look, if you ain't ready to speak on it, you ain't gotta."

"Nah, it's cool. Just - seeing them like this reminds me of how things used to be."

"I get it. A year before everything changed, I'd just come out to my family. Was too sacred to do it in person, so I posted a pic of me and Viv on all my socials."

My eyes widened and Max chuckled. "In 24 hours, I went from being a Daddy's girl to the black sheep."

"Dang, I'm sorry."

"It's cool. To this day, I still don't regret it."

Max's eyes weren't on me, so I followed them. We both grinned as Viv winked at Max. "One thing this ERA shit made clear to me was you gotta live like every day is your last. And with Viv beside my side, I know I'm gonna do that with my last breath."

I wiped my eyes. "I'm real glad Mother found me. Being here with y'all...it means a lot."

When Max brought a hand up in a fist, I did the same. Bumping fists with her, I nodded. "That's what's up."

"Well, let me get back to my ol' lady."

I couldn't hide my giggle before asking, "What you mean, ol' lady? Ain't it all our birthdays today?"

"Yeah, but since Viv was already two years older than me - I calls her my ol' lady."

Even though we were a good 20 meters away, Viv's frown was clear as she glared in our direction. As Max shrugged, I kept laughing.

Viv's frown deepened, and as I looked on, her entire face twisted into something that chilled me to the bone. A shrill scream ranged out while Viv sprinted to Max. She was just inches away when I felt a wetness land on the side of my face.

"MAX! MAAAX!"

Max's left hand caught my sight and when I finally registered what I saw, Max was on the ground. It looked like she was having a seizure. Both Viv and I kneeled down to help her up, but Max tightly coiled her fists together and it seemed like she had to fight with everything she had to move her head from side to side. The pain in her voice latched onto my still heart when she grunted out, "No! S-st-stay back!"

Blood oozed from the top of Max's shoulder and my eyes locked onto the barbed wire and black cords that held her legs and feet together. More footsteps could be heard from behind, but I couldn't take my eyes off of Max. She was looking straight ahead, and then in an instance, her eyes went to Viv. Neither of them got the chance to say another word as Max's body lurched forward. Cars screeched and honked while I tried to block out the heavy thumps that followed.

"MAX!"

When I turned around, four ERAs were doing their best to keep Viv from chasing after whatever took Max. Each of them gritted their teeth as they struggled to hold on to her. The kids from before were also screaming as more ERAs appeared and disappeared with them.

Soon, we all saw several red, white, and blue semi pickup trucks race through traffic. While blasting their horns, the trucks veered onto the sidewalk and gunned it toward The Garden. Above me was Luna and the rest of the aerial team, which I thought would never be necessary.

If only I knew how wrong I would be. All the ERAs on the roof worked in small groups of threes, guarding each other from behind as the ones in front sprayed the trucks with heat. Before ducking down like the others on the ground did, I desperately grabbed Viv's hand and shouted, "Please! We have to survive to get Max back!"

I just said the first thing that came to my mind, but seeing Viv's eyes focus on mine, I took the moment of her not resisting to pull her down and under the bench with me.

The other ERAs that once held Viv nodded and made their way toward the pickup trucks. I heard the rattling sound of chains reach my ears as I watched a pack of hunters jump off the back of their pickups with some dude ERAs. Their white shirts had the words 'Sons of Light' scribbled in bold across all of their chests as they proudly held their bows and rifles. The dude ERAs each aimed stunners and didn't waste time as they squeezed the trigger at the nearest women ERAs in their sights.

My rage grew with every scream and round of shots I heard. Looking over at Viv, she squeezed my hand, and I met her glare as I lifted the table with my right hand. Keeping my hand on the end of the bench, I inched it closer until I held the middle of it with both hands. "I can't do much, but I can for sure watch your back."

Viv stared hard at me and raised her chin as her eyes surveyed the scene around us. "Okay. Move when I move."

Without another word, Viv unclasped one end of her set of chains from around the loopholes within her denim shorts as she tugged them free. Then she did the same with the chains that were around her waist and my eyes grew from the size of them. Each chain set looked to be at least four feet long, maybe longer. Viv then reached into her back pocket and produced a small lighter. Before I could ask what the plan was, Viv flashed off to a section of The Garden and then back to me. Kneeling, I mimicked her movements while looking around at the others laying out Sons of Light and those punk ass dude ERAs. The overwhelming smell of gasoline filled my nostrils and from the corner of my eyes, I saw a trail of the liquid traveling forward.

Our ERAs stepped together silently behind the invisible line as a guy in a Son's of Light shirt shouted, "What? That's all you bitches got?"

"Yeah, I think they done homie." a male ERA taunted.

Only one of us stayed across the line of gas. I didn't even see when Mother arrived, but once I heard her voice I knew she had been on the scene for a minute.

"No, you bitches are done."

The low chill as Mother spoke rooted me to the spot. "Now!" she commanded.

Viv and three other ERAs sent their chains sailing into the air, just before Viv struck the lighter to the ground. The bright, warm light blazed around us in seconds, almost making it hard for me to see what happened next. But I saw it.

Mother had caught the chains, two in each hand. When she struck them out, the way someone would giddy up on a horse, the two dudes closest to her cried out as they fell to the ground.

Several men started shouting at once.

"Oh shit!"

"Everyone back! Back to the pickups!"

Mother's voice was still low, but now had more of a dark amusement to it when she growled. "Where y'all going? I'm just warming up."

Not waiting for an answer, Mother flicked the chains over her head, twisting them against one another as they hit the ground. The flames caught hold of each one, and as the fire inched closer to her hands, Mother stalked forward. Extending her arms, she whipped the chains to the few guys that weren't fast enough getting in the back of the pickups. Three of them wearing Sons of Light tees were dancing in the flames as they tried in vain to climb onto the back of the pickup.

In their panic, the burning hunters spread the fire to the other guys and male ERAs in their ride, causing the driver behind the wheel to swerve off the road and into an abandoned building. More bodies hit the ground, as the ones that got caught in the fiery chains ran without caution into the others who couldn't get out of the crossfire fast enough.

The wreckage wasn't enough as Mother continued to move forward with ultraprecision, lashing the chains near every Sons of Light follower and male ERA in her way. I couldn't take my eyes off of her as blood splatter on top of her head wrap and the sound of flesh ripped through the parade of carnage she left behind.

Their hollows echoed in the now dark night, and for the first time in months, I fully allowed the fiery rage to dance throughout my whole body. One truck revved up and rolled out, but not before tossing something large and wrapped in what looked like a tarp onto the now deserted traffic lanes. The figure rolled a few times before coming to a stop, and when my sights zeroed in closer, I found myself crouching over the wrapped mass before the thought exited my mind.

Slowly, I placed a hand on the wrap to inspect it further and gagged. Max's body was covered in burns. Her hands were bound together with barbed wire, and her mouth sealed shut by black duct tape. Moving fast, I ripped enough of the barbed wire off with my teeth, ignoring Max's muffled screams as I unraveled the rest. Once I did and moved to get rid of the tape, she shoved me away.

She brought her hands together into a triangle shape, using her fingernails as a blade to slice through the tape. The second her mouth was open, Max spit out a small object into her hands.

"What the hell is that?!" I rushed out while whipping my head around for any incoming from the Sons of Light or male ERAs.

"I don't know, but when them muthafuckas shoved it in my month, they all were grinning like a kid on Christmas morning." She answered with a scowl on her face.

The circular object in Max's hand was about the size of a fist and looked like it was made out of some kind of metal. When I tried to peer closer, I heard what sounded like the timer on one of those old cooking timers that my mama used to use. When the sound echoed louder, the metal object in Max's hand became brighter. From a dull greenish blue to a burnt orange. I didn't know much, but I could feel the icy pricks spread down on my spine. This was bad - like real damn bad.

Max's voice was hoarse as she whispered. "I think it's a bomb."

Hearing more footsteps getting closer, we looked up to see our squad catching up to us. I glanced up at Max one last time before we both turned around and yelled as loud as we could.

"Fall back! Fall back - now!"

Just as I saw Luna showing the others yesterday, I took off toward The Garden. Running while waving my hands frantically in the air, I kept shouting, "Stay back - please! FALL BACK!"

"EVERYONE DOWN!" Max screamed.

A piercing ring grabbed my attention, and I followed it just in time to see Max launch the small metal gadget into the air. It looked like the fourth of July when it lit up the pitch black sky. My legs shook before giving out completely, leaving me on the ground.

As I felt wet streaks on my face, Viv and Andrea appeared in my sights. Andrea spoke first, "Why did you go out there by yourself like that?"

When I didn't answer, Andrea questioned me again. "What was it? What made you go out there without a vet?"

"I needed...I needed to do something." Was all I could think to reply.

A gust of air blew past me and Viv's cries of joy filled the air, along with the space where my heart used to beat. My eyes stung, but this time I didn't care as I watched Viv hug Max and gash her wrist open. It was the first time I'd seen an ERA feed from someone directly and it must've showed, as Max locked eyes with me and winked.

"I ain't mean to scare ya like that ol' lady." Max said casually while holding on to Viv. "But our new eager eagle here got to me just in time."

Splashes of red painted the ground in front of me as I shook my head. "It wa-it was - my fault they..." I had to tell them, to apologize for distracting Max during the party, but the words wouldn't come out as I tried again. "Viv...it-it was...my fault they got Max. I-I'm sorry."

Andrea spoke first. "Maya, none of this was your fault." I listened to her chuckle as she brought her hands together before tossing something toward me. The metal object glistened in the dim street lights as I caught it with ease. I reached out and found a spike brass knuckle ring in the palm of my hand.

"That's for the next time you wanna pop out and go off without a vet." she told me with a grin.

Andrea patted Viv on the back as used her vamp speed to disappear into the night, leaving me alone with Max and Viv.

Lifting my head, I met Viv's stare and I swear she looked at me as if I came down from the sky with wings and a halo.

"You brought my baby back to me. Thank you, Maya." Viv said softly.

Max kissed Viv on the cheek, and the two stared into one another's eyes before she glanced my way again. "You did some big brave stuntin' today, newbie. Thanks."

As they strolled away, another pair of feet appeared in front of me. They were covered in dirt and blood and it wasn't until the person sat down did I realize who it was. Gently, Mother wiped away my tears, and as she brought me into her chest, fresh ones fell. I tried to pull away, tried to get away from her watchful eyes.

After seeing what Mother did tonight, I couldn't stand the thought of looking weak in her presence. But she held me tighter, swaying me while rubbing the small circles along my back. That was when the whole dam broke. I stopped holding back the misery and sorrow that was beating around in my chest and wailed as more bloody tears left my eyes.

"I know you hurting now, and that's okay." Kissing the top of my forehead, she continued. "You did what you couldn't do for your friend back then, and I am so proud of you, Maya."

Hearing those words, I reached my arms around her neck and cried harder.

"You 'gon be okay. Today you fought back and survived. Now let it all out baby girl."

* * *

Almost two weeks had passed, and Viv and Max were still off guard duty. Mother had asked me to feed them and to keep them up to date on the new schedule and training, so I saw them more than everyone else. At first, I wondered why I'd been tasked with this responsibility, since Viv and Max heard everything with their enhanced hearing. Until one day, as I was leaving their apartment and caught the two of them whispering in the corner, in between kisses. They thought I had sped out, but Mother had also made me promise to walk at non ERA speed more, so I wouldn't forget how to when around them in public.

"She's doing better, not as jittery as she was after what happened." Max murmured against Viv's neck.

A moan slipped past her lips when Viv nodded. "Yeah, but let's pretend to need a break - at least for another day or two." Viv suggested.

"Another day of no work and having you to feast on? Abso-fucking-lutely."

That was when I realized the check ups hadn't been for Viv and Max. They'd been for me. I wanted to be offended, but honestly wasn't. My first rumble in the concrete jungle did leave me shaken up, but like Mother said - I'd survived. And now I was ready for more.

The next day I didn't have to use the spare key to go inside the apartment, as Viv was waiting for me with the door open.

"We can set our watch to you, eager eagle."

"I heard you and Max yesterday." I blurted out.

Her face stretched out into a grin. "I hope you didn't stick around to hear everything that went down in here."

Flashes of them kissing entered my mind, and I dang near tripped over myself before sputtering out. "N-no! Nah - not all that. Just the part about me."

"Then you missed all the good stuff, not-so-newbie." Max said as she came into view behind Viv, placing a kiss on Viv's shoulder.

I struggled to think of something else to say, but luckily I didn't have to as Viv asked, "Whose training you these days?"

"Luna offered, but I said no."

Viv let out a hoarse laugh and grinned while staring at me to explain. "So now I'm with Andrea on the second shift."

"Good. Good. Learn all you can to help keep The Garden safe." Max chimed in.

Viv went to lie back down on the couch, but before she rested her head, she glanced over at me and paused. When she sat up and locked eyes with me, I swallowed hard.

"I will. With my last breath, if need be." I vowed before adding, "I-I know I've only been here for a little while, but y'all have been nothing but kind to me. And I hope to be at least half as good at protecting The Garden as y'all have been."

As I stood in between the open door to their apartment, both women grinned at me before Max extended a fist in my direction. Another dull warm ache where my heart used to be deepened when I dapped her up.

* * *

I doubt anyone was surprised that I volunteered to be on patrol with Viv and Max later that day. When our first shift was over, I jogged up to Viv with a plan to get stronger and more fearless faster. "Hey Viv!"

When she turned around, I pointed at the small matching blades that were strapped to her thigh. Each knife was almost invisible along the outside of her dark leggings and narrow, with a small gold band holding them in place.

"I was wondering - could you show me how to use those? Think they'd be good for me if I ever have to square up with someone."

These?" Viv confirmed, glancing down before returning my gaze. "My twin Katanas?"

Viv looked down at the blades that securely fastened to her thigh before smiling my way. "You got good taste. Let me get you one of my spare sets and I can teach you a few moves tonight."

As we made our way back to her apartment, Viv stopped walking. Worried that she figured out why I really asked to learn how to use the blades, I started working on what to say to her next. But when I looked up, Viv's attention was on the small crowd of folks walking on the sidewalk. Some were at the stoplight, others were sitting at the bus stop, and about a handful were heading toward The Garden. She and Max shared a look as they both took off toward the crowd.

"Go get the next sisters on patrol - now!" Max hissed, not taking her eyes off the crowd.

I took off in the opposite direction and took the stairs two at a time to Pearl's apartment. Before I could knock on the door, she swung it open.

"Viv told me to come get you. She didn't say why, just for you to come."

Pearl's eyes practically bore into mine before she asked, "What did y'all see?"

"There was a group coming toward us, mostly guys."

"How were they dressed?"

I blinked as I tried to remember clearly, and when I did, my eyes widened. "Like the dudes that showed up on our birthday."

Several more women appeared behind Pearl and in unison, we all began to sprint to the front of the complex. Without breaking her stride, Pearl issued out orders to the group. "Aaliyah and Monica - back. Brandi and Vica - to the sides. Give signals when in place."

No one spoke as we reached the final stairs, each of the women splitting up to go to their assigned posts. Pearl and I reached Max and Viv's side as we took in the scene. Four men were about 6 meters away, all wearing dark shawls and masks, except one that stood a few feet away from the others. When he moved closer, Viv unsheathed her Katanas and growled low.

"We are here to speak with the one called Mother. Is she here?" The man in front of us asked when he came to a stop.

Viv raised the blades and clanked them together four times. I knew the signal and held my breath as we all waited for the others to respond. Two seconds later, I closed my eyes when I heard Brandi's melodic cry fused with the low tapping of pipes from where Aaliyah and Monica were in the laundry rooms.

When none of us spoke to him, the man raised his hands over his head. Pearl whipped her tiny spiked chains from around her waist, and two of the men took a step forward. That was until the guy ahead of them turned toward them and whispered, "It's okay. Stay still."

He turned to face us again and removed the black shawl from his head, exposing brownish red locs. They softly landed at the middle of his back, and I couldn't help but admire how the color contrasted beautifully with his blueish midnight skin. It'd been a minute since I found anyone attractive, with me trying to survive the new world I live in. But this man left me wanting more than the taste of blood, and that made him even more dangerous.

"My name is Tome." He said before adding, "We don't mean to alarm you, but our sources told us that this is where we could find the one known as Mother."

"Just who are these sources?" Pearl asked, though the edge in her tone made it clear that one wrong answer would put all four of the men in the ground.

Tome looked back to the three men and faced us before answering. "A man named Willie. From Willie's Wings and Thangs."

"Then you know the relation between Mother and Willie?" Max barked. "What is it?"

"There is a closeness, as one has toward their sibling. Though the two are not related by blood."

"Viv, Pearl, Max - it's okay."

Hearing Mother's voice from behind, I wanted to turn and see her. But that would have earned me an early morning half marathon run without my ERA speed as punishment from Viv, as we are all taught to never turn away from anyone when in a hostile situation. Especially a male ERA.

"This Tome has more than words to back up his request."

Mother glided slowly past me, and closer to this Tome guy. When she stood in front of him, Mother held out her hand and I heard the smile in her voice. "At least Willie was smart enough to give you protection."

Tome flashed a pair of the whitest teeth I'd ever seen as he tugged on the front of his neck and handed Mother something. A small smattering of colors from the rainbow danced in my sight for a second as she wrapped the jeweled chain around her wrist.

"We lost four games of Spades before he would give me that gem." Tome explained, a soft smile spreading wider across his face.

The laugher that broke out from Mother's lips filled the otherwise deafening space. "Pearl, Viv, and Max, please let the others know I'll be talking with Tome." Mother said.

Max started to interject, but Mother tilted her head. "I am fine. He won't harm me."

Pearl narrowed her eyes at the trio that still stood on the sidewalk. "What about them?"

"My men will keep their distance, if that will make you feel better." Tome offered.

All three women scoffed.

"If y'all could be trusted to do that much, we wouldn't have half the problems we do now." Viv spat out in their direction.

"If they move, Maya will send out a signal." Mother said plainly before looking at me. "You know which signal I'm talking about, right?"

With everyone eyeing me, all I could do was send a brief nod in Mother's direction.

"Good. Then you three can go."

I eyed Viv and Max before nodding again as they turned with Pearl to leave. Part of me wanted to ask so badly why Mother had me stay, but with my mentor and friends gone, I had to focus on the assignment given. My eyes surveyed the men in front of me. So far, they hadn't moved since Pearl, Max, and Viv left, and I prayed to the heavens that they would stay in their lane.

I put my hands in my pockets to keep them from shaking and felt something move inside. The cool gunmetal from the spiked brass ring was a much needed reminder of what was at stake for me in this moment. Thinking back to the night Andrea gifted me the ring, I took two deep breaths and slowly released them while eavesdropping on Tome and Mother's conversation.

"Like I said, my name is Tome, and I'm here to share critical information with others like you."

"What do you mean, 'others like me'?" Mother asked.

Tome extended a hand toward the bench a few feet away and Mother followed. As the two of them sat, I went to follow, but stopped when Mother glanced my way. My eyes traveled back to the men still standing on the sidewalk as Tome spoke again.

"Other ERAs are forming communities like the ones you have here. They want to get all those in charge to meet and change history - the right way this time."

"Thank you, but to be honest, I ain't doing this for no recognition. Not even to try to change history." Tome and I listened as Mother continued, "I just want to help those left heal and build a safe place for everyone."

"That is precisely why you have been sought out. You are already doing what needs to be done for your people." Tome further explained, "That is how we learned of you, Mother. I am here on behalf of a group of leaders that have gotten together with one goal - to bring people from all over the States together to ensure peace between ERAs and non ERAs."

"What's the name of this group of new leaders?"

"They are called the Final Watch."

Mother glanced at Tome and asked, "How did you find out about them? This Final Watch?"

"I was selected as a representative for the Final Watch after helping two of the founding members stop a turf war in my state. It was something similar to what happened here last month."

I continued to listen silently as Tome spoke. "I go in search of others with the same goals and mindset as The Final Watch and invite them to the summit."

The question was out of my mouth before I could stop it. "What you mean, the summit? Like one of them bible study trips?"

Tome chuckled, but didn't move other than to look at me. "I am extending an invitation to the leaders of every community I can for them to travel to what used to be the nation's capital. That is where we will meet and hopefully begin once more."

"What is the point of doing something like that?" Mother asked with a hint of curiosity now in her voice.

Tome explained, "We are going to the former capital to end it - officially. It is our aim to keep the peace, raise awareness, and put an end to the government that allowed this to happen in the first place."

"That sounds all well and good, but I don't want to leave my communities without the people I've trusted to keep them safe."

"No proper leader would, Mother. That's why we have sought only you out. And you can bring a select few from your team to accompany you."

The two stared at one another, and Mother seemed to think over Tome's words. When she said nothing, he continued. "Your presence would be much appreciated. So everyone that comes to the summit can hear you speak about the communities you have created. The people need to see that we can and want to live together - in peace."

Mother looked between me and Tome, and I watched on as she stared out at the tenants and folks passing by while they all went about their day. When she sighed, Mother spoke evenly. "Can I talk to everyone here and give you an answer later?"

Before Tome spoke again, I met Mother's stare. "I can get the others together now, Mother." I volunteered before quickly adding, "If you want me to."

When she smiled at me, I knew at that moment I would follow her anywhere. Being here at The Garden, even though it'd only been a short time, made me feel good. More than good - it gave me purpose. And that was worth even more than I could imagine. My friends and family from before were gone, but I was still here. I am still capable of doing something with myself. And if I can help Mother, then that's what I want to do.

"Thank you Maya. Please ask them to meet with us so Tome can tell them more about this summit."

With her request, and my newfound determination, I left Mother and Tome to go and prepare the others.

Reunited

Kem

BEING FROM THE SUNSHINE State, I thought I'd be able to handle this heat. That turned out to be just one more lie I told myself once we got word that we'd have to get to the old capital by foot starting in Maryland. Though at that point we'd been from bus to bus for so long that I convinced myself it'd be good to just walk anyway. Now that we were finally within the vicinity, I was dog ass tired and longed to be back on a bus. For the third time that afternoon, I swiped sweat from my brow and continued trekking along with the other volunteers. Up ahead, we all noticed the subway tunnels and picked up the pace to keep up with our director and team leaders.

Once inside the empty subway station, a collective sigh of relief could be heard throughout the group. I made sure to untie my twists from the bun they had been in, so that my hair could cool down a little while we continued on our way to the next place we'd be sitting up camp. As my thoughts went back to my auntie at home, Ella, my assigned buddy for our journey, spoke. "It's so trippy being in here. I've never seen this place completely empty before."

"Right?" Another volunteer called out and then added, "When we was in high school, this line was always dang near full."

"Guess no one wanted to risk having their throat slashed by a mob of angry Black vamps."

Boos and groans echoed throughout the space, and I knew they were aimed at Chad, the poster child for bitter bigots everywhere. His parents happen to be pro-ERAs and funded the Worldwide

Humankind Organization. I remembered seeing him sulking behind the auditorium when the organization arrived at school two months before I graduated.

After receiving flyers and wristbands from who would later be my team leader, Heather, I went home and started doing more research on the organization. Once I knew they were legit, I told auntie Tammy that I was going to sign up and join them for the summer as a medical assistant intern. She wasn't happy with my decision, but since I'd turned eighteen a few weeks prior, she couldn't say much about it.

"Whatever, whatever. Y'all know I'm right." Chad continued.

I sighed. "Well, you're partially right."

"Kem!" Ella shouted in disbelief. "Don't tell me you agree with this piss nepotist trick?"

Chad barked toward us before I could answer her, "Watch your mouth - welfare baby."

"You say that like it supposed to mean something, you dumbass wanna be jock." Another volunteer called out from behind.

A few others began talking at the same time as Ella raised her voice. "Yeah, I might be from the projects. Just like the majority of us here. But ya 8 by 5 ass don't wanna get into how folks like you made 'welfare baby' a thing in the first place, now do you?"

Cheers erupted around us before the other team lead and Heather flashed their bright neon yellow LED flashlights into the crowd. "That's enough, everyone. We're almost to the meeting point, so focus on that instead of the old days."

Everyone knew that 'the old days' was code for 'stop talking about shit that'll upset the trust fund baby', so we all quieted down.

Ella leaned close and whispered smugly into my ear, "Doesn't she mean 'facts'?"

I coughed to keep the laughter from coming out of my mouth. Though once I got myself together, I remembered my original point from what was said a minute ago, "The city closed these tunnels in an attempt to reduce the widespread panic and looting that began days after the vaccine outbreak. And with this being close to the nation's capital, it made sense, as the government wanted to try and keep a sense of unity among the citizens."

"Are you sure you wanna study pre-med when this all ends?" Ella asked.

My stank face was in full effect as I looked her way. "What's that supposed to mean?"

"I'm just saying - you sound like them news reporters just before the stations stopped airing."

Rolling my eyes, I went back to focusing on the trail in front of us. "It ain't a crime to stay informed of the world."

I almost paused as the phrase left my mouth, but somehow managed to keep moving. That was one of my mama's favorite sayings back in the day. I hadn't heard anyone other than her use it.

I cleared my throat. "Anyways - after Washington closed down all the subway stations, other cities did the same. That's why they're deserted."

"It worked out for us, right?" another volunteer said before adding, "We got this whole new underground railroad and shit 'cause of their fear and ignorance."

Ella and I stared at each other before she shook her head in disbelief. "I just know they ain't just say that."

"Yeah, they did. Outloud and everything."

Silence fell over the group for a while until Heather stopped. She waited for everyone to circle around her before speaking. "Okay, we are now entering the last rest stop before arriving at the old capital. Everyone, please make sure you have everything you need in your kits."

Ella and I sat down and removed the straps from our backpacks. I'd already checked my supplies during our last stop, but just to be sure, I went through the count with her. We all had two standard and fully stocked first aid kits, radios, batteries, a flashlight, and bottles of water.

As everyone went over their kits, Heather and the other team leader reminded us of our goals while in attendance at the summit.

"We are to assist with the medical care of non ERAs and provide information as it comes in through our radios. Do NOT try to take on anything beyond your training. If a situation calls for more than the CPR and other life saving training you all have received, radio us immediately. If we can't get to you in time, we will walk you through the situation using your WHO guidebooks. Questions?"

When no one responded, our team leaders looked at one another and walked to the opposite sides of the station. "Okay, teams! Please line up in front of your assigned team leader and wait. We'll be leaving shortly."

Ella took my hand, and I looked up at her. Her face seemed calm, but after training side by side with her for almost three months, I could see in her eyes the anxiousness that hid there. Hell, I was scared too.

"We really out here?"

"Yep."

Ella surveyed as the other twelve groups went to their designated spots before letting out a shaky breath. "You ain't nervous?"

"Nope."

"Bullshit."

I cut my eyes at her. "If you knew I was already, why ask?"

"Cause I thought you'd have one of your inspo quotes or something to say like you always do. Damn sis."

"Well, I don't keep TED Talk one liners in my pocket, Ella. So can I please have just a few more minutes of quiet before we get into Lord knows what?"

She didn't say anything, but I could feel Ella's eyes on me. When I stared back at her, she shook her head. "You know, you kinda rude when you nervous."

We both looked at one another before breaking out into small laughter.

"I guess so."

A yellow light flashed up in the air just as Heather spoke again. "Okay! Let's move out everyone."

* * *

I didn't know what to expect once we left the subway station, but it wasn't this.

There were rows and rows of huge orange and red tents, all lined up in front of buildings that had clearly been abandoned for some time. If I had to guess, I'd say they had been that way since the subways got shut down. Blacked-out windows still had banners that read 'Be back in November' hanging up. It was now March, and with fewer and fewer members of the old congress still away, it was safe to say that no one would be returning to work here anytime soon.

People walked in and out of one of the smaller tents, where hip hop music blared from, but other than that, the area was quiet. ERAs waved at us, some even flashing their fanged grillz while going about their day. About thirty steps into our walk, we noticed two dusty gray tents side by side one another with a large red cross at their openings. There was a smaller sign at their entrance that read, 'Welcome WHO, and thank you!'

"Damn, the ERAs set all this up for us?" Ella asked, to no one in particular.

The other volunteers wordlessly followed our team leader as she marched us to the tents. When we all stepped inside, a woman dressed in all camo gear and a black shawl seemed to float over and smiled at the sight of us.

"We heard you all arrive minutes ago, but I didn't want to scare you off." She chuckled to no one in particular before adding, "It is so good to see so many of you!"

When the woman in front of us reached up to remove her shawl, I was left in awe as she showed off her completely shaved head. A red blade encircled by a wreath tattooed on the right side stood out against her light tanned skin, and I couldn't stop staring as she came closer to our group. With her hands in a prayer gesture, she bowed slightly.

"I'm Canary."

Our team leader walked over to Canary and returned the greeting. "It's nice to meet you, Canary. I'm Heather, and this is my team. The others should reach the front of the line soon."

Canary looked out at us and nodded. "Good! Well, you all must be tired from the journey. Please come inside and get some rest."

Her words were just what we all needed to hear, as everyone on our team rushed further into the tent. Once the others showed up, a few volunteers hooped and hollered.

"Yo! Is that a game station?"

"They have beds! BEDS!"

Another woman, about my height and easily the biggest afro I'd ever seen, approached Canary. The two shared a smile as they watched everyone's reaction. Ella grabbed my hand and led me to the makeshift operation section. My eyes widened at the sight of five hospital beds, monitors, and rows of medical supplies in steel cages.

"Luckily, we haven't had to use this space since setting up camp here a month ago."

We both turned around to find the woman that joined Canary standing behind us. She greeted us the same way that Canary did.

"I'm Ella, and this is Kem." Ella said excitedly.

"Please call me Sam."

Finding my voice, I finally spoke up. "Nice to meet you, Sam."

Her eyes stayed on mine as she answered. "Kem, the pleasure is all mine."

I cut my eyes to Ella, who let out a small squeak while looking straight ahead. Following her gaze, I had to take two steps back as Sam now stood directly in front of me. Not sure what to say, I watched as she tilted her head and a grin spread across her face. Part of our training included how to respond when engaging with ERAs, so I followed the WHO guidebook and steadied my breathing as she stood close. Honestly, I wasn't worried. Mainly due to there being no reports of ERAs attacking anyone without being provoked first. Maybe that was why I even found the guts to smile back at her.

After what felt like forever, Sam finally removed herself from my personal bubble. "I'm sorry, Kem. It's just, well, you look extremely familiar, and I let curiosity get the better of me."

"I-it's okay, I guess." I told her. A thought occurred to me, and before I could stop myself, I asked, "Do I remind you of a loved one from your past?"

"Kem!" Ella whispered harshly, "You can't ask an ERA that!"

There was nothing in the WHO guidebook that even suggested what Ella had just said was true, so I ignored her and kept my gaze on Sam, who now was grinning even wider than before.

"You could say that," she answered before adding, "I suppose you will see soon enough."

The merriment in Sam's eyes as she walked away left me more than a little confused. I almost didn't hear Ella snapping her fingers until they were right in my face.

"Hello? Houston, we have a problem!"

"What?"

Ella stared at me with a hand on her hip. "I thought you had some sense!"

I couldn't get a word in as she continued, "Why you out here asking ERAs about their families? When you know most of them ain't been back home and probably don't know if theirs is still around?"

Her last sentence stung as it opened a wound I was doing all I could to heal. Facing away from Ella, I willed myself not to cry before turning back to meet her glare. "Last I checked, it said nothing in the book about asking ERAs about their family. And we both know I read the entire guide - which is more than I can say 'bout you!"

Catching my breath, I made my way from Ella to go back outside, but stopped as I noticed Canary and a small group of women make their way toward Heather. Curious, I watched as another woman emerged from the middle of the group and my knees buckled. I almost refused to believe who I saw until her laughter throughout the crowd reached my ears and pierced my heart.

She looked just as she did the last time I saw her. Except now beads adorning her mid shoulder locs. Closing my eyes, I was mentally transported back to the night she left me. She thought I was asleep when she kissed my forehead, but I wasn't. That all too familiar scent of cinnamon and spearmint still haunted me long after I saw her quietly close my bedroom door two years ago.

"This is Mother, the one behind setting up each of the medical stations your teams will use. She'll also be traveling with us to the summit."

"Mother?" I choked out.

When she glanced my way, I watched as she took a step forward. Her eyes seemed to glow red as she stopped herself from moving. Everything around me went dead silent while we held each other's stare.

"Damn! She looks EXACTLY like you Kem! I thought you was an only child?"

My eyes remained focused on the woman they called Mother as I barely whispered, "I am an only child."

When Mother slowly extended a hand in my direction, I struggled to breathe. The need to get some air took over, forcing me to march toward the front of the tent. I swung the divider open and welcomed the blazing sun onto my skin. Two big inhales and exhales later and I still couldn't gather enough strength to stop the tears from cascading down my face.

* * *

Days passed, and I still hadn't spoken to Mother. And I didn't want to. Even as I watched her direct and guide the others on the many procedures that were in place for getting people to and from the summit safely.

I couldn't help but notice her presence though. When we weren't in meetings or doing hands-on training. She was good, I guess. Of course, since Mother did work in the nursing field since before I was born, she would be adequate at all this. Flashbacks of seeing her hovering over diagnosis and treatment books with a cup of coffee came to me, and I instantly shook the memories away.

Looking up, I found all the other volunteers laughing as Mother voluntold two ERAs to join them as their practice dummies. One of them tried to refuse and Mother asked them calmly, "Maya, do you want to be of help to these volunteers, or lead the team on guard duty outside tomorrow?"

I peered up as the ERA crossed their arms and Mother continued, "And I hear it's gonna be over 90 degrees out there tomorrow, too. The choice is yours."

She then handed the ERA a small set of cards before strolling away with a tiny smile.

Yeah, I remember her giving me choices like that too. And as I looked over at this Maya chick, all she could do was glance at the volunteers and sigh. Soon several of them started asking her questions, and she crossed her arms before clearing her talking again. "I know Mother said I was y'alls practice dummy or whatever, but at least let me pick a card to act out before y'all start shouting out possible symptoms. Dang!"

As they all laughed and skimmed through their guidebooks, I tried to ignore the feeling of someone staring at me. Ever since Mother appeared, folks from both WHO camps have been watching me. No one other than Ella said anything, though. They just stared like I was a ticking time bomb, waiting for me to go off. And it was starting to piss me all the way off.

Heather introduced us to the ERAs that would be accompanying us to the old capital and explained how we'd be helping the ERAs break down camp in two days. The next day would begin our trek to the summit, as it was scheduled to take place in four days. I couldn't wait to leave. At least while walking, people would have something else to watch besides me.

For the second time that day, I felt like I couldn't breathe. Every inhale and exhale was like I was pushing flames down my throat and that my head was going to burst. Dropping the medical chart book I was pretending to read, I made my way to the other side of the tent where the large gallons of water were kept. I listened to the whispers from the trio of volunteers while picking up a paper cup and pouring water into it.

"Mother is a real badass!" one volunteer said excitedly. "Can you believe she been frying Sons of Light dudes while giving the ERAs basic medical training?"

"I know, right? Wish my mom was that cool!"

I dropped the paper cup in my hand, earning the attention of the three volunteers. They all stared at me, slacked jawed before scurrying away without a word.

Yeah, I can't wait to be on the road to the old capital. Away from Mother and all her fans. No sooner had I thought the words did I see her. She was making her way toward me, and I immediately started walking away.

"Kem Anita Greene, stop right now."

I hate that she could still stop me in my tracks by saying my full government name, but when I heard it, I froze. Though when I turned around, I saw Mother fidgeting with her hands before placing them behind her back. Auntie Tammy told me once that she only broke out that move when really nervous.

"I...It's good to see you."

Looking up at her, I quickly glanced away.

"H-how have you been? I mean, you look well." Mother tried again. "How's Tammy doing? She taking care of herself?"

"Yeah, well, now she is." Seeing her eyes widen, I rushed out an explanation. "Auntie Tammy slipped a disc last year, but that seemed to make her slow down. She said she's retiring for real this time next year."

I heard her laugh and even though I didn't want to, I joined in. Auntie Tammy has been saying she's gonna retire since I was in middle school. She said it so much that it became a running joke in our house.

"With me going away for college soon, I really want to see her retire."

"You going to college?" Mother interrupted before asking another question. "To study pre-med?"

I nodded, "Uh-huh. That's part of why I'm here. WHO is giving us volunteers scholarships for completing training and helping at the summit."

Mother looked straight ahead and rapidly blinked her eyes before whispering, seemingly to herself. "That's real good, baby girl, real good."

Ella suddenly appeared between us, crossing me to get to Mother to hand her a tissue. "Here, Mother."

Seeing Mother nod to her friend and Ella grinning up at her, I mumbled out, "This is bullshit."

"Kem!" Ella harshly whispered. "Can't you see she is-"

"No! This is all bullshit! You here leading the charge, like you got your doctorate in medicine or something." With all my feelings bubbling to the surface, I felt my face grow even hotter as I spat out, "Now you in my face, asking about my life after you left?! You didn't have to sign up for the damn booster shot!"

I narrowed my eyes at Mother, who stepped closer to me.

"Baby girl, I..."

"And stop calling me that! No one has called me that in years and I hate it!"

Soon Mother's eyes matched mine before she spoke again, this time her voice more authoritative than it was a moment ago. "I know you mad, and you got reason to be. But life is too short to be hating anything."

I frantically waved my arms in the air, almost tumbling over my own two feet as I sarcastically replied, "Oh, is it now? Thanks to the old government, life ain't what it was no more. You ERAs will probably live forever!"

Thinking back to the last time I asked Auntie Tammy about the woman that stood in front of me, I cackled, "Is that why you never tried to come see us, uh? Too busy starting over to be bothered with the jit and lame ass sister you left behind? I bet-"

My head flew backward, as the sting from Mother's slap traveled across my entire face. When I righted myself to look her way, Mother's head bowed downward to the ground. Her left hand shook violently, and seeing it told me I'd gone too far. Even in the old days, she never once struck me. Soon I had more shame and guilt to contend with then I knew what to do with as Mother's voice reached my ears.

"My first thought when I climbed out of that pit was to get back to you." her voice sounded so far away as she continued. "And I did go back."

Glancing back at her, I waited to hear more. But before that happened, Ella interrupted us. "Mother, the ERAs need your help in confirming the logistics of the trip."

We both stared at one another, and my face fell as she walked away.
* * *

Days later, we were all back on the road and with the scheduled breaks, our medic team was expected to arrive at the old capital within eight hours. Never thought I'd be so glad to have to walk for a whole day, but with all eyes still volleying between me and the woman everyone's calling Mother, I found myself longing for the distance.

The first two hours were the most peaceful hours I had since arriving at the camp. Me and Ella trekked along and she did most of the talking. Telling me stories about her family, exes, and her plans to open a rehabilitation near the apartments she grew up in once she graduated and finished her residence at Brown Medical Center. I could feel eyes on me right after our first break and I knew it was Mother watching us.

"She's been keeping her distance. But I definitely noticed her behind us since leaving camp." Ella told me as we shared a bottle of water.

I said nothing, tossing the empty bottle into a nearby trash can.

"Maybe you should-"

"I don't have to do anything." I said quickly, "Except get to this summit."

Ella scoffed while adjusting her backpack. "Dang! You ain't gonna be so snippy. I was just trying to help."

"Don't need your help. Not even as a teammate." I replied smoothly, picking up the pace. With a few feet now between us, I kept my attention on the road ahead. Which is why I didn't realize who was right beside me until she spoke.

"Isn't that young lady your partner for the summit?"

I said nothing as Mother went on. "If you leave her behind, can you honestly say you did everything that was expected of you for this event?"

My brisk walk became a stroll as her words rattled around in my head.

"You can feel whatever you feel about me, but pissing off a teammate, one of the few friends you got, ain't the way to go about dealing with your feelings Kemmie."

"Don't call me that!" I shouted.

The other groups and ERAs continued walking by us as I stopped. Hot, angry tears threatened to fall down my face, even though I swore I wouldn't shed one more tear over this woman. Meeting her stare, I glared. "You think 'cause you got a whole parade of folks worshiping you that I'll do the same? Well, I won't!"

Mother opened her mouth to continue, and I cut her off. "Auntie told you not to go to that damn clinic! And you went anyway! Why? For a few dollars?"

"Kem, I-"

"No! You don't get to tell me shit!"

Mother's face narrowed. "I get that you're mad, but don't forget who you talking to, little girl."

Upon hearing her thinly veiled threat, I dropped my backpack. "Oh, how I wish I could! For years, I tried to forget you! Just to stop the aching in my chest!"

Seeing her eyes fill with tears, mine overflowed and ran down my cheeks while I slapped my hand to the center of my chest. "I ain't mad! I'm HURT! I MISSED YOU! I wanted my ma- you to come back home! But you never did. Now I finally see you, only to find out you been playing superhero all over the place. Being superwoman for everyone except your own damn family!"

The silence hung in the air between us for a minute before she dropped her head. Wiping her face, Mother kept her head down. "Do you remember what I started to say the day before yesterday? I really did go back home."

"Why didn't-"

Her voice rose slightly as she interrupted. "I heard you, now hear me."

I forced myself to remain quiet and waited.

"The first night, I didn't know what happened to me, or what I was. So after making it home, I watched you and Tammy from outside. Y'all looked so happy... So safe."

Red droplets splattered to the ground beside Mother's feet as she continued speaking. "I didn't trust myself not to kill you that night. So I drove away. To keep you and Tammy from seeing what I became."

When she finally raised her head, my heart wanted to hide from the sight of pitch black eyes swimming in blood and canine fangs that took over her face. Walking forward, she took two steps in my direction before turning away.

Most of what I saw on TV before studying as a medic volunteer looked like something out of a movie, which made it easier to process. That was until the person I loved more than anything stood in front of me, completely vamped out. All the stories I'd heard about folks seeing their loved ones come back and being something else didn't add up to me. But I know if she had come into the house looking like she did just now, I wouldn't have been the same afterwards.

Wordlessly, I jogged back up to Ella and I said nothing, even as the wind picked up behind us. I knew it was her again without turning around. We all fell into step along with the others. But an apology hung on my lips, and the need to say the words out loud got heavier and heavier in my heart as the groups moved further along.

Turning around, I looked at her. "I-I'm sorry. For what I said earlier to you." Taking a deep breath, I continued, "I didn't get it before, but I swear I do now. And I'm sorry."

She looked at me and nodded. "Make sure you apologize to Tammy too. When you get back home."

Crinkling my nose, I asked, "Why I gotta apologize to auntie too?"

"You forgot what you said about her already? When you was talking out your neck to me?"

Thinking back to what all I said early, I immediately cringed as the words flashed across my mind.

"Mmm hmm. Tell her what you said and that you're sorry."

"I wi-"

A melodic cry rippled through the group, and Mother held out a hand to silence me.

Ella piped up, voice low. "What is it?"

"Hunters." Mother said, her voice low as she stared out into the clearing.

I couldn't hear anything, but the ERAs were moving at warp speed. All the nonERAs were forced to huddle together and Mother went to stand guard with the others. Though before she was too far away, I grabbed her wrist. Images of when I last saw her, before life changed flooded my mind. And I couldn't stop myself from saying what I didn't back then. "Please... Please don't go."

Her smile was just like it was years ago. Until her eyes grew bigger and quickly shut. When they opened again and traveled down, I followed their movement and my heart dropped to the bottom of my stomach from the sight of the harpoon as it bore through her chest.

"I love you, baby girl." Mother whispered.

Before my screams could leave my mouth, she roughly pushed me backwards, and I landed hard on the scorching concrete. Then, in horrifying slow motion, I watched as bright white lights flashed wildly from inside the harpoon that was still lodged in the middle of her chest. My eyes bulged even more when Mother moved at record-breaking speed away from me, until she was no more than a mirage in the hot sunny sky.

ERAs encircled me, and the other non ERAs close by. I heard others shouting commands to one another as men on dirt bikes and doom buggies roared through the crowd.

The sounds of chains and gurgled screams reached my ears, and I opened my eyes in time to see the ERAs flip over the vehicles that the gang of men rode in on, trapping many of them under. Soon gasoline filled the air and the temperature rose, making it harder for me to breathe. Shrieks and squeals ranged out as burning liquid rained on the men. Several spears that were attached to the dirt bikes had fallen onto them, impaling their crew. And the same white light that I saw in Mother's chest could be seen again, this time by the dozens as the bloody hunters tried in vain to escape the traps of their own making.

Four of the men did somehow make it from under the trapped dirt bikes and doom buggies, only to be quickly lassoed back into the herd by ERAs on the outside with chains. I looked on from the safety of the ERA dome I was cocooned in as more groups of men fell to their knees and loudly pleaded for mercy. When their pleas were ignored, they clawed at the chains around their necks, even as more chains appeared. And with two chains in opposite directions around their necks, the ERAs each yanked in unison. Their bodies fell forward, with their now detached heads flapping slowly onto the ground before coming to a stop after being lopped off.

My mouth opened, but I said nothing as the scene in front of me ended. Instead, I wrapped my arms around my shoulders, rocking back and forth. The blazing sun beat down on my head after several agonizing minutes. I could hear voices shouting my name, but I didn't want to hear them. All I wanted was to return to the moment where I had the one person I missed most back in my life again.

Hands roughly grabbed my head and shoulders as I stood upright. Locking eyes with Ella, I waited for her to say something, but she didn't while blinking back tears.

"Dammit! Y'all alright?"

Finally opening my eyes, I saw Maya and Viv jogging toward us. They were part of Mother's camp and I knew who they were really looking for as their gazes went past my shoulders. Everything that happened played back in my mind, and I joined Ella in my sad attempt to not cry when I answered their quiet question out loud. "Sh-she saved me. Some white rod thing h-hit her and..." My throat wanted to close completely, but I forced the words out, "...and pulled her away."

A moment of silence passed between them as Viv glanced away from me and off into the distance. "That's what Mother has always done."

When Maya approached me, red tears threatened to fall down her face. She stared at me intensely as her bottom lip quivered.

"You saying they lit her up? Is that what you're saying? Th-they lit... lit up..." I looked on as Maya clenched her jaw and wiped away the red streaks from her face. Maya's voice was raw with emotion as she finally asked, "Did they light up Mother?"

Viv looked between the two of them and then faced the area where the hunters had arrived from. "She never told anyone her name from her life before. In all these years. Never let anyone call her anything but Mother."

The younger girl, Maya, spoke, "I asked her once." I looked on as Viv whipped her head toward Maya who continued, "She told me that in her life before she had one child. But after the outbreak - she couldn't go back to them."

I felt both of their eyes on me and for the first time since arriving in Washington, I didn't want to run away from their stares. Taking in two slow and shallow breaths, I stared back at Viv and Maya. I didn't fight the tears that fell as I choked out, "Her name was Pam Greene, and sh-she... She was my mama."

Our trek was silent throughout the night, even after we arrived at the final destination the following day. Everyone in our group found a reason to stay close to one another, from helping set up to making sure we knew where we were to be stationed during the summit tomorrow. Hours passed and before the day ended, a small group of men wearing cloaks approached us. Immediately I hung close to Maya, who softly told me, "This is Tome. He's the one that invited Mother to the summit."

A Black man with dark brownish red locks stepped forward and nodded. "Hello again. Is Mother with you?" Tome asked before explaining. "I wanted to introduce her to more of the community leaders that have also arrived."

Next to Viv, another woman appeared and I watched as they entwined their hands while moving to stand in front of me. Maya straightened her stance when she answered. "We lost her yesterday. In a hunter attack."

A crimson tear fell from the corner of her eyes, and Tome took a step toward her as she wiped it away. Glancing at them each, he slowly bowed his head as his eyes took me in. "I am sorry, truly. Mother was an inspiration to us all."

Another couple, a woman in a wheelchair and an Asian man wearing green framed glasses, stood behind Tome's men. They locked eyes before the two came forward and Tome whispered to them. When the couple glanced up again, their eyes barely reached mine before the man addressed us again. "I'm Ji-soo Nam, and this is my wife, Dr. Jazz Sinclaire. If you all need anything, please do not hesitate to allow us to help."

Since I knew I could never get what I needed, I bit the inside of my cheeks while the others murmured some words to him I barely heard. And when they left, Maya led me to my tent for the night. She stayed with me as I fought to sleep, finally closing my eyes when she took her lukewarm hand in mind.

PREPARE FOR THE WORST and hope for the best was the mantra all throughout the summit, but it really went down without any more lives lost. The amount of ERAs that were on security saw to that much. And all me and Ella ended up doing for the better part of the event was taking care of a few non ERAs that were dehydrated, and dodging questions about what things were 'really' like being surrounded by ERAs for so long.

It wasn't til the end, when I heard the loud cheers and hollering from the crowd did I realize it was all over. We all were going back to whatever homes awaited us. That was when my heart began its descent to the bottom of my stomach. Checking my supply bag as Ella and I waited to hear from Heather about our trip back to Florida, I noticed Maya staring at me from across the medical tent. No sooner had I locked eyes with her did she appear a meter from me. I jumped back from the sight and she nervously brought her hands down to pull at the sleeves of her windbreaker. "Sorry, Mother kept trying to tell me to stop speed vamping..."

Maya's voice faltered as I looked up at her. "I'm sorry - I"

I shook my head. "It did hurt, hearing you talking about her just now, but I'm okay." She tilted her head at me and I sighed. "Okay, so I'm not okay. But I have to try, right?"

"Not with me." She said softly. "In fact, that's why I'm here. I want to go home - with you."

"What?" Ella and I said in unison.

"I want to leave with y'all." Maya clarified, "I already got Max and Viv to okay it, as long as I call weekly and check in physically twice a month. But they told me I have to ask you too."

I was genuinely curious when I asked, "Why? Why you want to leave with me?"

Maya stared down at her hands and wrists again, rubbing them together before stopping and looking me directly in the eye. "Because of Mother - your mama - I learned to fight back, to protect those that care for me. So I want to see what her life was like - before all this happened."

When Maya paused, a more determined glint in her eyes appeared. "I wanna find out what I'm supposed to do next with this second life of mine. And I think going to Florida is the first step to doing that."

Even if I was gonna say no, there was no way I could after hearing that truth from one of the last people who got to know mama. Also, a part of me was curious about who my mama became after not returning home. I knew Maya would eventually talk about her - just like I'd hoped to again someday.

"Okay." I said finally.

Maya's grin filled her entire face, showing off her dusty rose cheeks that left me wondering just how old she really was before all this went down.

"Okay? You for real?"

"Yeah, I'm for real." I told her. "You can come back with us."

"Yes! Thank you so much!"

She engulfed me in a tight hug, dang near cutting off my air supply, until she stepped back. "I'm sorry - I forgot how much stronger I am when excited." Maya explained sheepishly.

All I could do was look between her and Ella and sigh. My lips tugged upward, and I imagined mama looking down at us. That thought helped chase away a little of the pain I felt, and to me, it was a promise of better days.

Four months later

IT FELT GOOD TO BE back home, even if it was temporary.

Auntie Tammy didn't change a single thing in my room while I was away at college, and I can't thank her enough for that. I took my time climbing out of bed, stretching my legs and arms once I was upright. Just before I left my room, I stared at the only fresh addition to my space - an eight by ten photo of me and the two most important people in my life at my high school's honor society celebration. I remember being so nervous that day, since I was selected to give the class commencement speech. After I did, I rushed off the stage and my mama instantly engulfed into her arms.

She planted peppered kisses that smelled like spearmint all over my face, telling me how good my speech was. When she released me, Auntie Tammy's arms replaced hers as she swayed me side to side and sung more praises. Before we left the gymnasium, one of my teachers offered to take a photo of us and I'm so glad that they did.

Mama's smile radiated as she and Auntie Tammy held on tight to the younger version of me. Blurs from the day leading up to the summit clouded my mind while I brought my index and middle finger together to my lips. As the last words mama said to me left my mind, I brushed my fingers along her face in the picture frame.

"I love you too." I whispered, making my way downstairs.

That first month after the summit, WHO made good on their end of our agreement, and I walked away with a four year partial college scholarship. By then, more people heard about what happened to me and before I knew it, I had three bodyguards, since Maya, Max, and Viv returned home with me, and school after school trying to get in touch with me before the semester started. After talking with auntie Tammy and meeting with the legal team that was overseeing all the cases from the vaccine lawsuits, I had made my decision.

Choosing to stay with my first choice, mama's alma mater at Bethune-Cookman College was easy, especially since it was in state. And knowing that the Lee Henry Ko-Ops would be providing us with a hefty ass settlement, along with footing the bill for all of my college expenses didn't hurt either. I didn't say much once I signed all the legal documents, but truth be told, I'd give it all up on the spot to have mama back.

"Morning baby girl!" Auntie Tammy greeted me with a kiss as I looked around the table.

Maya sat down with a full plate of pancakes, and Viv wasn't too far behind with a pitcher of orange juice. Ella was already digging into her breakfast of pancakes, eggs, and bacon, and I couldn't blame her. Auntie Tammy was always the better cook between the three of us, and I missed her meals while living on campus. After saying grace, I grabbed a fork and dug into the fluffy stack of pancakes.

"Is that all you gonna eat baby?"

Looking up, I watched as Maya slathered peanut butter and honey over her pancakes. "Yes ma'am."

Auntie Tammy's side eye was in full effect as she scoffed, "I wasn't talking to you! We all know you 'gon outlive me, so stop with that ma'am mess already."

Viv hid her smile as she poured herself and Max some orange juice. When Viv walked out of the kitchen to join Max, I felt Ella's stare and glanced up to see her rolling her eyes. "But yesterday you checked me for not saying it - that ain't fair."

I shook my head as auntie Tammy's hand playfully pushed the side of Ella's head, "I know you ain't talking bout life ain't fair lil' girl. Just eat your breakfast in peace 'fore I find something for you to clean."

Once the chuckles died down, we all did just as Auntie Tammy asked. Until Max's voice called out, "Ms. Tammy! The first commencement is starting."

My breakfast was the last thing on my mind as I followed auntie and the others into the living room. Since the summit months ago, I mostly avoided all ERA related news. But this commencement was the exception, as it was the beginning of the new council.

The new ERA was starting. I just wish mama was here to see it.

We all huddled on each side of the couch, with Auntie Tammy and me sitting next to one another. She kept her eyes on the television screen as she grabbed both of my hands, gripping them tightly.

Thousands of people stood their ground in St. Augustine, Florida, bearing the sweltering heat to be present for this life-changing moment - ERAs and non ERAs alike. The cameras showed the conflicting divide between the many people there, as some held signs calling for peace and others in red Sons of Light t-shirts chanted in the distance for the return of the old regime.

Auntie Tammy vigorously shook her head, "Those folks ain't never gonna act right! After all that's happened, they still out here hoping for hate to make a comeback."

"The new assembly said they would, which is why they chose to have their new offices there." Ella replied before quickly adding, "Dr. Sinclaire says it's a consistent protest in and of itself to rebuild on such a historical site that illustrates where cultures began and how the old ways are now being made anew."

Everyone turned to look at Ella, clearly shocked, and she scoffed, "What? I can't follow the news now?"

Viv spoke first, "Ain't nobody say that. We just surprised you know so much about it, that's all."

"Max," Maya looked between Ella and me before asking seriously, "Should I go to school too? Cause it sounds like it's doing ya girl Ella some good."

I swatted Maya's shoulder when Ella narrowed her eyes their way, causing both Viv and Max to laugh.

"I'm just saying! Ain't nothin' wrong with being aware of what's going on in the world." Ella huffed before turning her attention back to the TV.

Both Auntie Tammy and I glanced at Ella, as mama's favorite sayings left her lips. Auntie Tammy softly smiled in agreement before giving her full attention to the TV. "You right baby girl, ain't nothing wrong with that at all."

Several cameras rounded on the newly appointed speakers. Both ERAs I didn't know about and pro ERAs that I had heard about online faced the crowd. One I remember very well, except she now donned streaks of silver in her fiery burnt orange hair as Ji-soo gilded her wheelchair to the center podium.

The cheers ricocheted until they raised their hand, quieting the audience.

"My name is Dr. Jazz Sinclaire, and I would like to sincerely thank you all for being a part of the first commencement of The United Council. As many of you are bearing witness, this United Council is made up of individuals that come from all parts of North America. And we recognize what this will spark in those who would do not think we are fit to take on the task of rebuilding this land. To those who would say as much, allow me to be the first to tell you that you are right.

Dr. Sinclaire grabbed the microphone from its stand and steeled her gaze out into the crowd as they murmured. With her other hand raised, she explained. "We are not here to rebuild, for this new assembly seeks to allow for its people a chance to birth something stronger, something bolder that others around the world will witness. There will be no crowning or coronation today, for this journey will not be pretty."

She waited for the crowd's applause to cease again as she continued, "Nor will be easy. In fact, rebuilding the world in an image that allows for all of us to live and thrive peacefully will be a never-ending and difficult task. But too many have given their lives for us to not see this through. It is for them, as well as all of you here today and watching at home, that we must come together and continue forward. And with that, I am honored to announce the first line of The United Council."

A well loved hip hop classic track boomed and rattled into the walls of their home from outside, as the neighborhood celebrated the news the best way they knew how. And as much as I wanted to join the party on the block, I couldn't leave the couch.

As Dr. Sinclaire called out the names of everyone on stage a thunderous applause welcomed each person. All of the people on the screen shined like a beacon of light for the community they represented. From inner city enby ERAs to indigenous women non ERAs. The hope that rose within my chest made it easy for me to wish that things would be alright someday.

And as I felt Auntie Tammy squeeze my hand, I vowed then and there to do all I could to make this new era the best one yet.

Thank You

WRITING THIS STORY, pushing myself to give you all something entertaining while also opening the door for meaningful conversations afterwards was no effortless task.

If you've enjoyed this read, even a little, all the hardships I faced during writing this would have been well worth it.

Please leave a review on your favorite website so that others may decide if *The New E.R.A.* would be a great story for them to get into.

And thank you for taking a chance on an indie author. I hope you'll continue to do so in the future.

Until next time,

K. McCoy

Coming Soon...

Hits Keep Coming
by K. McCoy

ALL JADE THORNTON HAS ever wanted was to write songs and play her guitar. But after a school recital gone wrong, she accepts that it will never happen.

Years later she is reunited with a former friend, the charismatic Nashone Daniels, who convinces Jade to chase her songwriting dreams again with the help of the music label, Guerilla Records.

Now entrapped with shady executives and petty artists, Jade realizes that one misstep could end her career before it starts.

But with the promise of an LP album on the line, will Jade be able to pay her dues, or will her songwriter dreams finally fade to black?

Say What You Wanna Say

(excerpt from *Hits Keep Coming*)

JADE MADE HER WAY BACK to the stage and froze at the sight of Joe holding what looked like her songbook in his hands.

Oh god! Please don't let that be my book - please!

She kept her eyes on Joe while quickly weaving through the empty coffee tables. Sure enough, the green composition book that she stupidly scribbled 'Musing Notes by Jade' on the front cover was in Joe's hands.

"H-hey! I didn't know you were back." Jade said nervously. Her hands immediately went to take the book out of Joe's hands. "I'll put this..."

Joe sidestepped Jade, his eyes never leaving the pages of her book. With her heart jackhammering wildly against her ribcage, Jade managed to whisper out, "Joe? Can I have that please?"

"Why you ain't tell me you can write?"

Afraid of what Joe was reading - or thinking - at that moment, Jade chose to answer jokingly, "Well Joe, most college students can read and write."

Jade's throat went dry as he stared at her.

Gone was the usually mischievous and warm hearted man she'd come to know and respect over the last few months. Joe's voice was stern when he spoke again, "Why you do that there?"

"Do what?"

"Try to be funny instead of answering the question I ask ya?"

Jade blinked at Joe before she tried to speak again. Knowing that he wanted an honest answer left her unsure about what to say.

"I-I don't know."

Jade's shoulders slumped before she looked down at her feet.

"I ain't mean to embarrass you baby girl, but Jade... These here lyrics are good."

Hearing praise instead of a lecture, Jade cautiously brought her eyes back to his.

"Really?"

"Yeah baby girl! You got some good hooks and stuff in these pages." Jade's beamed.

He really said I was good? Really?

But Joe's praise was short lived when he continued, " But why this the first time I'm seeing it. By accident, no less? Why you writing all this down and not telling no body?"

When Jade went back to looking at her feet, crossing one pair of kicks over the other, Joe hit her with another round of questions. "You thank that's how all them famous songwriters got to where they at now? Hiding from everybody and keeping their words tucked away in books?"

When she didn't answer, Joe looked at the composition book again and handed it over.

"You got a gift. More than that - you is dedicated to learning how to better yourself. A lot of folks say they can do what you do, but they never do."

Joe pressed his lips together before he let out a tired sigh. He shook his head as he finished, "But I see you Jade, and as much as it pains me to say it, you ain't ready."

Jade looked up at Joe with her mouth open. "W-what? But you just said-"

"Being gifted and being ready to go into the world with your gifts are two different thangs."

She glanced down at her composition book, trying to ignore the stinging that was building behind her eyes.

"How long you had that there book?" Joe asked

Jade looked at him again and answered. "For few years."

"And I bet ain't nobody seen a word in there 'cept you. Right?"

She thought back to her junior year of high school, when Nashone read out loud lines from the same book when he'd found it by accident. *I bit his head off. Maybe Joe's right and I just can't do this.*

"Now, ain't no reason to be looking all long in the face. You just need to be honest with ya self. Why you write in that book and not say what you feeling?"

Jade knew the answer, but wished like hell it wasn't true. Though since walking into Clarity's all those months ago, she finally felt safe enough to say so out loud.

"I'm scared." she muttered softly.

Joe stared at Jade for a beat before motioning for her to sit on the stage carpet. Once he did the same, sitting across from her, he asked gently, "Whatcha got to be scared of?"

Years of being an easy target for folks to make fun of flashed through Jade's eyes. Memories she wanted to forget of family members teasing her and classmates clowning her as she passed them in the hallways. No matter how hard she tried to forget, her mind wouldn't let her. And she hated it.

"I'm scared to share what I feel... cause when I tried to in the past, people laughed. And I don't want to try to fit in anymore only to be hurt again."

Joe slowly nodded. "So you keep writing your thoughts in that book, getting it all just right. For what?"

She brought her eyes up to Joe, not sure how to make sense of what he was saying.

"Putting yourself out there ain't never easy, even when you get my big age." Seeing Joe puff out his chest, causing Jade to giggle.

"But I'mma let you in on a secret. You don't do it for the crowd - you do it for *you*." Jade opened her mouth to speak, but Joe waved a hand in the air as he went on, "Yeah, it sholl is nice when what you have to say is well received. But life don't work like that baby girl. Putting yourself out there in this big ole world to get hurt is part of the life experience."

Jade tilted her head and fought hard to not turn her lips downward, "Even if hurts?"

"*Especially* if there's a chance you'll get hurt. That's called being brave. And the ones that get it will come to 'preciate you more for putting yourself out there."

Silence filled the cafe as Jade thought over his words.

"From what I read in your book, you got plenty to say. So, if you want a crowd to hear it - you gots to be brave and share it with them baby girl."

Don't miss out!

Visit the website below and you can sign up to receive emails whenever K. McCoy publishes a new book. There's no charge and no obligation.

https://books2read.com/r/B-A-VWLI-KZWQD

Connecting independent readers to independent writers.

Did you love *The New E.R.A.*? Then you should read *A Dove's Cry*[1] by K. McCoy!

[2]

Can love bring a saint and sinner together?Jerome Grant Junior, a preacher's kid and Tasha Daye, an aspiring photographer, become friends after a night of celebrating at a local gentlemen's club.Desperate to leave town after a family betrayal, Tasha tries to keep her feelings for Jerome locked away.Though as their individual dreams begin to take flight, they both are forced to make a choice - will they take that leap of faith or part ways to pursue their passions?

Read more at https://authorkmccoy.com.

---

1. https://books2read.com/u/m0BRjy

2. https://books2read.com/u/m0BRjy

Also by K. McCoy

MAGIX
MAGIX
MAGIX: Melodic Whirlwinds

Standalone
A Dove's Cry
A Season to Love
Cupid's Kiss
Holiday Bliss
Doves Cry Too
The New E.R.A.
Hits Keep Coming

Watch for more at https://authorkmccoy.com.

About the Author

K. McCoy is an independent author who enjoys writing across several genres.In her many years of self-publishing, she has traveled around the world, crafting stories based on real-world experiences, combined with hopeful possibilities. Using the knowledge gained within her authorship, K. McCoy now speaks to others virtually and in-person on a variety of subjects within the author community. And through those workshops, she helps authors write drama filled, heart gripping, and authentic stories.As a serial hobbyist, you can find K. McCoy studying other languages, tinkering with an old camera, or trying out a new Yoga pose when she's not writing or working on another bittersweet yet somehow still loveable story.You can find out how to connect with K.McCoy by visiting her on all socials under authorkmccoy.

Read more at https://authorkmccoy.wordpress.com/.

Empowering dreams. Inspiring success.

About the Publisher

be a muse productions, LLC Established in 2024

A creative publishing company that looks to uplift independent authors and promote their stories to diverse readers.

Read more at https://beamuseproductions.wordpress.com/.